POWDER

A Deadly Addiction

BlaQue

STREET CHRONICLES

Acknowledgements

First and foremost I want to thank the MOST HIGH for giving me the gift of scribe. Without me putting GOD first there would be no BlaQue!

Next I want to thank my parents Dever Drummond Jr. (R.I.P) & Yvonne W. Drummond! You both instilled in me that I could do and be anything I wanted. When I was child, it all seemed so cliché. Who knew you were right... I really could do what I wanted! Thank you for believing in me and making sure I always believed in myself.

I know I say this in every set of acknowledgments, but he is the reason I keep on pushing my pen! Dever Giovanni, my son, my world, my muse and inspiration. You are and always will be the best work of art I have EVER created. I love you!

My sister Yvette Drummond and my cousin Keena Thomas, I love you two more than words can express! I hope you are proud of me the way I am proud of the two of you!

Bryan Evans, I don't even have to say it, you already know what it is...Til Death Do Us Part!

Cecelia Parker and my mentor Authoress Shari Barnes, This book is dedicated in your honor. You ladies have become very important to me because you tell me like it is! You teach me something new every single time we talk and your wisdom and love guides me through this process! Ms. P, Thank you for lending me your son's name and letting me pick your brain on Nigeria! You made this book possible! Sharuuuuunnnnn if no one knows who you are they will! Red LOVE is on its way and it will be number one! I am claiming it! Thank you for pushing me! Without you there would have been no Authoress BlaQue and that's REAL!

Chanda Allen, Chandra Armstead #SAYLESS We are STILL the FLATS! No one will EVER change that!

Ianthe "Pajay" Milton my crazy twisted friend you are the bomb! You and Shamia Cummings pushed me... I started from the bottom NOW I AM HERE!

To my Kush Boys Family ya know what it is KB/KG4L!

To my friends, family and readers and groups who have rocked with me from the very start: Keonna Randolph, Qiana "QD" Drennen aka TWIN Thanks ladies! Charli B. Tisha C, Darnell and Nikki G, Head, Mary G, Nikkeishia P, Monica F. Shawnda H, Natoya T, Denise W, Denise H, Sharlene S, Jonathan S, Barbara M, Rowena P, Pamela P, Tiffany W, Papaya, Rita and Charles King, Just Read Book Club, Got Books, Urban Ink, Princesses Read Too, Tammy's Readers, BFSB, Literary Divas, Nook Readers, Bayou Divas, Sisters into Reading, Urban Reviews, SLYCE, NAS, BRAB, FBA, Team True Glory, The Takeover, Sistah's on Lit, OOSA, and all of the groups I talk to on a daily basis, thanks for all your support!

To my author family: Treasure Blue, Mack Mama, Eyone Williams, NeNe Capri, Jimmy DaSaint, Gavin ML Fletcher, Tammy Capri, Vanna B, Clever Black, Fabiola Joseph, Thank you for your wisdom and helping me understand this business!

Last but not least my G Street Chronicles Family: Chandra Armstead, Honey, Tnicyo, Katavious Ellis, Mz. Robinson, Sabrina Eubanks, Tya Love, Janie DeCosta, Amy Warren Patterson, Cachet, Fire & Ice, Aaliyah

Shalawn, Lynise, V. Brown, Kim Carter, Meek Mill, David Patten, Latorria Jetson, and Chunichi, WE ARE TAKING OVER THIS GAME one book at a time!

Boss Ladi & COO, Shawna A. and CEO & Boss, George Sherman Hudson, I say it all the time, thank you for believing in me!

Lastly, as I said before to every hater, naysayer and wrong doer, WATCH ME WORK!

I hope you enjoy my twisted tale Powder: A Deadly Addiction. Lyfe Jennings said it best; God don't like ugly and he ain't to fond of pretty neither.

Now step into the world of Samantha" Powder" Underwood and Fade 2 BlaQue!

~BlaQue~

CHAPTER ONE

Powder

My name is Samantha Underwood. With a name like that you would think I am everything I am not. I should have been rich and had everything my heart desired. I should have had men lacing me in ice and catering to my every whim and need. Instead, I wasn't shit growing up but a black girl trapped in a white girl's skin. I guess you could say I became a product of my environment. I grew up in the hood, and I didn't know anything outside of the ghetto that my poor, white trash parents half-assed raised me in.

To make a long story short, we didn't have shit; and the only difference between me and my friends and neighbors I grew up with, was the color of my skin. My skin earned me the name Powder, but my hustle and gangsta eventually earned me my respect. I can't front, in the beginning I was afraid of my surroundings. A little naïve bitch like me didn't know I was different from the people I grew up with. I had the same story they did. My parents were fucked up and strung out. They didn't want to do shit but get high. I was tested time and time again because I wasn't black. I didn't see the difference in my skin color like everyone else in the hood did. I struggled just like they did. I wondered where my next meal would come from like them, and I stayed mixed up in more shit than enough; just like my peers did too!

I had the same problems as everyone else. My parents weren't shit! Both of them were dope fiends. They didn't care about anything but their next high. If they didn't have the money to get high, they were looking for ways to get the money to get high. There were plenty of times that they couldn't rustle up the money for a fix, so they were would end up sick, and that shit was depressing to watch. To top it all off, they were thieves. They were quick to rummage through the little bit of stuff I did have to make a quick buck. That fact alone kept me mixed up in some shit and in a fight with a bitch! They were always putting their greasy hands on something that wasn't theirs.

My mother, Elizabeth Underwood, was a shell of her former self. The drugs had taken her over so bad that she never knew which end was up, unless it came to her getting high. She had lost her job, her desire to work and her will to live. My father, Ryan, introduced her to heroin because he was a low-life piece of trash that manipulated her. He told her it would take the edge off. She went along with whatever my father told her to do, including making porn and selling it on the internet. Even that got old because she was a junkie, and not too many people I know want to see a dope fiend doing something strange for some change, unless you are a complete pervert. My mother got on welfare and somehow managed to keep a roof over our heads though Section 8 in this rough neighborhood. Other than that, she was totally useless to me.

It was nothing for my father to go out with promises of doing the right thing by trying to get a job. My father's idea of working was stealing shit from the Safeway Food Store on Alabama Avenue. The bum had the nerve to stand right in the store front and sell the customers the same shit he had just stolen; right in front of the security guards no less. I was never surprised when my father would go missing for a few days. I would always find out that he'd been caught stealing shit by way of posters stuck in store front windows warning folks to call security if they saw my dad's face. Or I would hear about him being locked up from some random female in our neighborhood taunting me that she had found out my junkie father was caught stealing again.

For a long time, I was the target of assault from the girls around the way. I dealt with them teasing me about my parents and their addiction, my fucked up clothes and my race. Those scandalous hoes chased me home every other day; if not every day. It was not uncommon for my neighbors to catch me ditching school because I didn't want to have a confrontation with any of them.

The fucking teachers acted like they were scared of the students half the time. They would never step in and stop the girls from picking on me. That ain't make me do shit but hate their asses too! It was a wonder I didn't drop out of school before I did.

CHAPTER TWO

Time To Take A Stand

I remember the day I dropped out of Martin Luther King Jr. Senior High School. This crazy bitch, Kira, who had made my life straight hell for the past two years, had succeeded in embarrassing the shit out of me once again. On my way to my locker, I saw her greasy ass give me the look she always gave me right before she started fucking with me. There was no way to avoid her either. She was posted up near my locker.

Kira was one of the popular girls in my neighborhood and I hated her. She had everything I wanted. She rocked fly clothes and her boyfriend, Marshall, was a 'get money' kind of dude. Kira stood 5'7" and her looks put you in the mind frame of the rapper, Trina. She would have been a pretty girl had she not had an ugly disposition towards white folks. Secretly, I wanted to be like Kira. I wanted to have the boyfriend who was deep into the streets and would lace my pockets. I wanted to be able to shop in the real stores, instead of having to settle for Thrift Store second hands. I wanted to ride around in fly whips and ball out of control.

"Bitch, you ain't shit but poor white trash," Kira said laughing wickedly.

I tried to ignore her and get into my locker, but this bitch was putting on a show for her friends. There was no hope for me escaping her. She had already let her hand be shown. She was ready to fuck with someone, and I was her target...again.

My fingers trembled while I fumbled with the combination dial on my locker. I wanted to get my shit and get as far away from Kira as I possibly could. I hoped like hell I would be able to get my task done without her tormenting me any further.

"Aye, did you hear me cracker?" Kira continued to taunt me.

So much for her leaving me alone.

"I don't want no problems with you Kira. I just want to get my stuff from the locker and go to class. I ain't got no beef with you," I said meekly.

I avoided making eye contact with her, scared that if I looked at her too long, she would take that as a sign of me wanting to challenge her. I stayed focused on getting my locker open and getting the hell out of there before shit got worse.

"Well, get your shit then and go! Ain't nobody stopping you! Matter of fact, why don't you get your shit and keep it moving right out of the fucking front door, white girl! Don't nobody want you here anyway!"

Her friends fell out laughing. This was their source of entertainment on a daily basis. They loved watching

Kira fuck with me and tear me down.

I finally got my locker open. I hated that our lockers were stacked on top of one another, so I had to stoop down to get inside mine. Grabbing my books for my next class, I thought I was going to escape the torture that Kira was going to inflict upon me because she had grown quiet. I couldn't back out of my locker fast enough before Kira slammed the locker shut on my head, which was partially inside. I howled in pain from the force of the metal smacking against my head. I tried to stand upright, but before I could, Kira kicked me forward with her foot. I practically fell into the locker, slamming the top of my head inside the locker this time.

The sounds of all of my classmates laughing haunted me as I scrambled to pick up my books that were scattered across the floor. Before I could get my shit, some of Kira's friends had taken my belongings and kicked them up and down the hallway like they were starting kickers on a football team. I tried to get past them and hurry to the principal's office, but they had me surrounded. I had walked right into a trap they had set for me. There was no doubt that Kira had orchestrated the whole show. She loved feeling big by making me miserable.

Holding my aching head, I attempted to get around them as they threw agonizing insults at me. I was standing in a crowd of people hurling threats and calling me names and Kira was the ringleader. Every time I thought I found a hole to make a break for it, the students closed the way for me to get out.

"Aye, fuck you white girl! You don't belong here!"

Kira chanted.

I ran around the crowd that seemed to close in on me until a girl name Shaunie moved to the middle of the group, moving my attackers out of her way. I don't know why Shaunie felt the urge this day of all days to step in and help me, but I was grateful that she had. Shaunie was just as popular as Kira, if not more. She was a beautiful, petite girl with a booming body. She was beyond beautiful, she was outright gorgeous. Her natural curly hair fell down to the middle of her back and her golden brown skin looked as if it had been kissed by the sun.

"Kira, that's enough! Leave her the fuck alone! She ain't done shit to you for you to be picking on her," Shaunie said defending me.

Shaunie grabbed my hand and led me through the gang of onlookers. She looked at each of them as if she dared them to disrespect her demands. The crowd parted and let us through. I cried the entire way down the hallway and into the girls' bathroom. Shaunie retrieved some tissue from one of the stalls and handed it to me to wipe my nose and tears which were both running like a faucet.

"You have got to learn to stand up for yourself! Until you learn to fight back, Kira and her friends are gonna keep fucking with you," Shaunie said, lighting a cigarette and hopping up on the sink.

I stared at her between the tears that were pouring from my eyes and stinging my bruised cheeks. She didn't know that shit was easier said than done.

"Powder, if you don't make them respect you now they never will. They will keep on fucking with you until they fuck around and drive your dumb ass crazy."

I lifted my eyebrow in confusion. "My name is Samantha, why are you calling me Powder and why did you help me?" I asked her.

"Would you rather I call you cracker or white girl? Powder seems appropriate for a bitch like you. You are white as snow and it reminds me of Powder. That's what I think I am gonna call you from now on. Besides it sounds better than Samantha. Samantha sounds corny as hell and you ain't never gonna get them niggas to respect you if you don't respect yourself. You understand?" she said between pulls of her cigarette.

I nodded my head like I understood, but in all actuality I didn't have a clue. At this point, I was willing to agree to anything that Shaunie said. She was the first person that had ever paid me any attention. It didn't hurt that she had also saved me from being further humiliated.

"Look, you are gonna have to stand up to Kira. If you don't, she is gonna keep on fucking with you. Is that what you want?" Shaunie asked, taking another deep drag of her *Newport*.

I was so afraid that if I had said something stupid she would no longer want to talk to me. So I agreed with everything she said.

"Powder, what are you gonna do to make sure that Kira and her little hoe bag friends don't fuck with you again? Do you even know how to fight?"

I decided to be honest with her about that question. I

didn't know how to fight, let alone stand up for myself.

"No. I don't know how to fight." I sniffled through my tears.

"Well, you ain't really got time to learn how to fight 'em, but if you get into some more shit with Kira, you have to be the one to make the first move. You have to strike first! That's the only way you will ever win," Shaunie said; her eyes were cold as ice.

"Here take this," Shaunie said, reaching into her *Coach* bag that no doubt was a gift from her dope slinging boyfriend, Rasaun.

She handed me a pair of brass knuckles. Those things were not allowed in the school and I wasn't so sure if they were allowed on the streets either.

"If she approaches you again, I bet these will slow her ass down." Shaunie smiled wickedly.

She tried to push the weapon in my hands and I wasn't sure if I should take them or grab my shit and run. I wanted Kira to leave me alone, but I didn't want any more trouble. Those brass knuckles were definitely trouble. I could fuck around and get expelled from school for carrying a deadly weapon, or Kira could beat my white ass, take the shit from me and whoop my ass with the very item that was meant to protect me.

"Look Powder, they ain't gonna give you any respect, so you are gonna have to take it! They're gonna keep fucking with you until you end up like one of those crazy mother fuckers we see on television that goes postal and shoots up the place. All I am trying to do is help you out before you end up dead or in jail because your ass flips

POWDER

out and takes out your anger on the wrong people!"
Shaunie said, hopping off the sink.

My eyes followed the knuckles as she went to slip
them back inside her high-priced, designer bag.

"Wait! I'll take them! Give 'em here," I said, still
somewhat frightened of what would happen if I were to
get caught with them. However, the fear of not having
them when I may need them scared me even more.

A smile spread across Shaunie's face. "Good! If she
comes for you, slip your hand inside your pocket and
put them on. Don't let her see them until it's too late. If
you do, she's gonna get away and try to snitch on you
and then you will go down for having a weapon. If you
do like I say, you will catch that bitch off guard, beat that
ass, and she will never fuck with you again! Simple as
that!" Shaunie said, snapping her fingers.

Shaunie handed me the brass knuckles. She put out
the cigarette and headed for the door leading out to the
hallway where we could hear the students hustling to
their classes.

"Shaunie, why are you helping me? I mean, what
do I owe you for this? I ain't got no money to pay you
for this." I held the weapon tightly in my palm. I had to
admit the weight of the cold metal made me feel better.
Knowing I had them made me feel safer.

Shaunie turned to me and smiled. "Powder, let's just
say I hate to see a good bitch down on her luck and it's
a favor amongst friends." She smiled as warmly as she
could. There was something sinister behind her smile.
I just didn't know what it was yet. Bitches like Shaunie

G Street Chronicles / 11

ain't just offer you their help for nothing.

"By the way, Powder, no one calls me Shaunie. Since we are girls now, I would prefer you call me Nee Nee." Shaunie smiled innocently. "See you around," she said as she exited out of the bathroom.

I spent damn near the whole day in the restroom attempting to avoid anyone who had seen the altercation earlier. I ducked into a stall whenever I heard someone coming into the restroom. No matter what kind of protection I had, I still didn't feel safe. I stayed in that pissy bathroom until the last period of the day. The only reason I finally eased out of there was because I had Mr. Weaver's class as my last class of the day. If I dodged his class I would definitely have a problem. His ass would see to it that a phone call was made to my parents. Not that I gave a fuck if he called them, and nine times out of ten they wouldn't care either. They were most likely too high to comprehend what he had to say anyway. The real fear came into play because Mr. Weaver would flunk my ass and I would be stuck in Martin Luther King Jr. High School another year and that was something I was not prepared to do.

I mustered up all the courage I could and made my way to class, hoping everyone would have forgotten about the incident at my locker earlier. My heart thumped in my throat. It seemed as if the short walk I had to Weaver's class was a lot longer than usual. The hallways were clear because the bell had rung. I prayed no one would see me creeping through the hallway. No sooner than I turned the corner leading to the hallway to my class, Kira and her clique ran right into me. They had obviously been skipping class and heading for the bathroom I had just come out of.

"Look ya'll! Here's this pale bitch now! I knew we would catch you sooner or later!" Kira laughed.

I don't know why I was paralyzed with fear. I just froze. Everything in me screamed, *run, scream for help*, but I didn't do any of those things. Instead, I tried to talk Kira down.

"Look Kira, I don't know why you don't like me 'cause I ain't got no problem with you," I said trembling.

Kira rushed towards me.

"I just don't fuck with you white girl or your junkie ass parents! Those dope fiend mother fuckers owe my man some cash and since they can't pay, I'm gonna beat it out of you like you owe me! Fuck you!" Kira said between clenched teeth.

I believed every word she said about my parents to be true. They weren't beyond getting their fix on credit and then have no way to pay their debt. They had fucked over one too many dealers in the hood. This time I had caught the backlash from it.

Before I could run, Kira charged at me and the fight began. Her friends cheered her on while Kira worked me over. I screamed out and everyone that came were only there to watch me get my ass beat. None of them tried to help me. None of them went for help. Instead, they cheered my attacker on. The teachers who finally got to the scene couldn't stop the fight; the crowd was so thick around us that they couldn't get through to break it up.

The crowd was screaming, "Fight! Fight! Fight!" while Kira beat me viciously.

I rolled over on my side and could feel the brass knuckles Shaunie gave me in my pocket. I struggled to get my hands in my jeans and grab what could save me from what was shaping up to be the ass kicking of a lifetime. Kira was too busy trying to grab my hair. She never saw me reach in my pocket. She hadn't realized what had hit her until it was too late. My fist connected with her ribcage. I barely did any damage with that blow, but it was enough to make her ease back a little. I knew she would recover fast because I wasn't used to fighting so the punch I landed had no force behind it.

Kira shook off the blow and swung on me again. Before the blow was able to connect with my face again, I sent my fist into Kira's nose. The sound of the brass knuckles cracking her nose was sickening. Something about the sound of her nose breaking, coupled with the sight of her blood pouring, it enraged me. I was sick of this bitch always bothering me because she had a chip on her shoulder.

The tables had turned and now she was the one who was begging for me to let her go. I grabbed her by her quick weave and yanked her around. I punched her wildly. I didn't stop until the school security was finally able to penetrate the crowd and get me off of Kira.

Even after they had broken us apart, I still wanted to keep going. Anyone who had ever wronged me, I was ready to take them on for making me feel like shit. The guards dragged me away. I could see pieces of Kira's teeth scattered across the floor, like she and her friends had done to my belongings earlier that day, and I was satisfied.

"Fuck you bitch!" I laughed while the guards secured me. I was going wild. In my mind anybody could get it, if they wanted it! As I was being led away, I saw Shaunie watching from a distance. She nodded her head in approval and gave me a knowing smile. I smiled weakly through my wild hair, Kira's blood, and my tears.

I knew right then I had what it took to fight back if I had too. I just didn't know my fight had only begun.

CHAPTER THREE

A Time For Change

It was bad enough bitches in the hood harassed me because of my race and taunted me with crazy ass names, but once I got older and started to fill out, shit just got worse. I went from a blond haired, blue eyed, flat-chested girl, to a stacked ass woman who was hated on daily. Folks thought I had paid for my shapely figure. I couldn't help that my ass sat up and my breast were full and perky. I guess you could say I had the shape of a sista. Which only gave hating hoes more darts to throw at me. They claimed I paid for my phat ass and busty chest. That shit was funny as hell to me being that I didn't have it like that to pay for surgery. My curves were all natural. I was surprised I even had curves. We barely had anything in my parents' home to eat to help me fill out.

The rude broads in my neighborhood could hate all they wanted because now that Shaunie had taught me the rules of engagement, I was never going to get my ass beat in the streets, or anywhere else for that matter, as long as I could help it.

Needless to say, I never went back to school after I beat the shit out of Kira. Even if I had gone back to try and explain my case, they would have expelled me anyway. To their knowledge, I had attacked Kira with a deadly weapon. They would have taken her side just because of the damage I had done to her with the brass knuckles. I said, "fuck it" and dropped out altogether. I wasn't going to an alternative school to have a bunch of bigger misfits messing with me. My parents could barely afford to get high, so there was no way they were going to pay for night school. Dropping out was my only option. The shit they were trying to teach me I ain't have no use for anyway. I was getting all the education I needed, and the streets were my teacher.

Since my body had gone from stick pin to brick house, the next lesson I learned from Nee Nee was the power of the pussy. At first, I started fucking dudes so I could eat. Then it turned to a lifestyle to get clothes to wear, fresh shoes and jewelry. You know...the essentials. I didn't have a choice but to fend for myself. My parents didn't even notice that I was no longer going to school. The only time they even noticed me was when they wanted something. I swear, as soon as I can get my shit together and come up on some money, I am getting out of here and I ain't never looking back. My parents don't give a fuck, so why should I?

Nee Nee had no idea that she was my first real taste of living a better life. After the fight in the school hallway, she and I become as thick as thieves. She showed up at my parents' home on First Street right after the fight to check on me, and I thought she had come to collect her knuckles from me since I wouldn't have to use them to defend myself from Kira and her crew anymore. The word on the streets was that Kira was laid up in the hospital trying to get her nose realign and getting her teeth fixed. When she supposedly got released from the hospital, her parents moved her out of the hood. No one knew what the fuck had happened to her. All they knew was that she had once gone to our school, was deemed a bad bitch courtesy of her boyfriend's money, and had ended up beaten into submission and sent to the hospital. That was the reputation that once was Kira.

Every time I thought of the damage I had done to her, a smile found its way to my face. I enjoyed beating that bitch's ass! She deserved it! Everyone knew it too! They were either her flunkies or stupid mother fuckers who followed behind her because of her boyfriend.

Don't get me wrong, I don't run around trying to fight every bitch who got a grudge against me, but I definitely learned to stand up for myself. I wasn't gonna just let mother fuckers push me around and fuck with me because I was in a fucked-up position with who my parents were and all.

I wanted nothing more than to be just like the girls I saw every day in the hood. I wanted to be accepted. I wanted to kick it with them, smoke, drink, party and the rest of the bullshit that normal girls experienced; but none of them would even give me a chance to show them I was just like them. Shaunie was the only person who fucked with me tough. I still don't know why she helped me that day in school. I had asked her several times about it and her answer was always the same. She was a friend, helping a friend. I got tired of asking her about it, so I left it alone. That incident was a year ago and far in the past. I was just happy to have at least one girlfriend. I finally had someone to hang with and tell my secrets to. I am eighteen years old and I never had one single friend; so I was grateful to finally have one.

I wiggled my jeans over my ass and fingered through my hair. A whole lot has changed in the last year. I was thinking of dying my hair from the deep, dark chocolate color to a strawberry blond, but I hadn't made up my mind on that yet. The contacts I rocked made me look like Kim K. I used that shit to my advantage whenever possible too.

I was supposed to be going out with some dude that Nee Nee's boy hooked me up with. I hoped he wasn't a busted-ass nigga trying to act like he was doing more than he really was. I have had my fair share of dudes trying to play me for a dumb female just because I'm white. They think I can't tell the difference between a Boss and a Buster. I definitely knew the difference and I swear Nee Nee better not be bringing a Buster to attempt to entertain me today. I could be doing other things with my time. My cell phone bill was due, not to mention, I am trying to move out of my parents' house. I needed to come up on some money quick.

My parents are still on their bullshit, but I'm hardly ever home to even care. I locked all of my valuables down before I left to ensure they would be there when I came back. My parents weren't beyond robbing me blind if I didn't make sure I hid everything that was worth something. The last time I left my shit unchained, they stole two of the bags my last boy toy, Rolo, had given me. Rolo was the reason I was broke now. I met him right after Nee Nee and I had become close. It wasn't anything serious at first between me and Rolo; just flirting back and forth. Then that led to us going out a few times and I started thinking this nigga was the answer to my problems. He was really spending money; so I thought if I gave him some pussy, he would spend more money and possibly make me wifey so I could get the fuck up out of my parents' house.

I had that nigga eating out of the palm of my hand and was damn near moved into his apartment uptown. Shit was going great until one night the police kicked in his doorway while we were fucking, and busted his ass on a Narc charge. Once he got locked up, I was ass out again. I was starting to think that there weren't any more men like Rolo left who believed in spending money and spoiling a bitch. I didn't have any money saved even though Rolo gave me money hand over fist. As quickly as he had given it to me, was as quickly as I spent it on clothes, shoes or some other shit that wasn't going to equate to shit in the long run.

I never thought I would be without Rolo or not have easy access to his money. The cops took it all when they raided his apartment. Rolo called me from the pen at least twice a week. I started off taking his calls until I found out he didn't have any money. I went from eagerly taking his calls when I thought there was a possibility of him having money or being able to beat the Narc charges, to sending that nigga straight to voicemail whenever I saw it was him calling from the inside. There was no fucking way I was going to run up charges on my phone, that I had to find some way to pay the bill for, while listening to some nigga cry about how bad he had it. Shit, I had it pretty bad out here too! Rolo should know, because he is the one who left me out here butt naked with nothing.

While I thought on how Rolo left me out here on my own, I continued to get dressed because I knew Nee Nee, her man Rasaun, and my mystery date, would all be pulling up shortly; and I didn't want to have them sitting out front too long in fear of them seeing my parents.

Sure Nee Nee had seen my parents. She seemed to never mind, but I damn sure didn't want anyone else passing judgment on me about my parents' drug habits. I wasn't shit like them, and I had no intentions of getting comfy in their house again. It was a hard pill to swallow having to cancel my plans on moving into Rolo's spot; but I refused to get reacquainted with my parents' trashy lifestyle.

Adding a dark eye shadow to my eyes, and glossing my lips, I finished getting ready. No sooner than I had blown a kiss at myself in the old mirror in my room that had seen better days, when my cell phone chimed, followed by a horn blowing out front. I knew that was

Nee Nee. I snatched up my bag and pushed my valuables into the chest and locked it. I ran into my father before I could get out of the door.

"Samantha, loan your old man a few bucks," he slurred. He was obviously sick and in need of his fix. His clothes were wet and stuck to his body. There was a foul smell emanating from him. I held my breath and kept it moving. I flipped my hair and walked past him like I didn't hear anything he said.

"Sam, I'm sick god dammit, and I need your help! Didn't you hear me?" He practically cried, holding his stomach. The monkey was surely on his back and he would do just about anything to make the sickness go away. I felt no remorse. Everyone had a choice in the matter. Either you did drugs or you didn't. My parents decided to do them, so I made a decision of my own too! I simply ignored them and pretended that I didn't see what was happening to them. They felt like drugs were better than being parents, so I felt like saying fuck them was more satisfying to me.

I bounced right out the door and to Nee Nee's boyfriend's Lincoln MKS that was sitting at the curb with gunja smoke pouring out the windows. I opened the door and slid into the back seat and noticed a familiar face. It was Marshall, Kira's boyfriend.

I was almost hesitant to get inside the car. I knew he didn't care for my parents because they had owed him money once upon a time. I was hoping this wasn't another set up to seek revenge against them. Rasaun, Nee Nee's boyfriend, caught me giving him dirty looks in the rearview mirror and he nudged Nee Nee to get her attention. Nee Nee turned around and passed me the lit blunt packed with weed. I raised my eyebrow at her in return.

"Powder, I want you to meet Marshall. Marshall this is Powder," Nee Nee said, making the introductions and breaking the awkward silence.

"I know who Sam is," Marshall said licking his lips like a hungry animal.

I fidgeted around in my seat. Marshall continued to watch me lustfully. I could see him from the corner of my eye. The way he called me Sam made me squirm. I had grown to hate when people called me Sam or Samantha now. I had done away with Samantha long ago and to me, she was dead. So whenever someone called me Sam they were lucky if I bothered to even respond. I took a few pulls from the blunt and passed it to Marshall's weird ass, who was still staring at me.

I had a serious bone to pick with Nee Nee and she was going to hear my mouth about this shit. She knew my history with this nigga's girlfriend. There was no way I should be out with him. The incident with Kira had happened over a year ago, and she was long gone; but I still didn't like the fact that he was the reason that she had a grudge against me in the first place.

After several blunts and a thirty-minute ride, some of the uneasiness left and Marshall wasn't staring at me as he had been before. His eyes were low and red from the weed. He was nodding his head to the 8Ball and MJG song that was thumping from the custom system in the car. We pulled up in front of some place called Fuji Mountain and Rasaun killed the engine.

"I don't know about you, but I am hungry as a mother fucker. This Purple gave a nigga the munchies," Rasaun said as he exited the car with Nee Nee quickly following suite.

I put my hand on the handle to exit the car and Marshall stopped me before I could get the door fully open.

"Samantha, I know I ain't your favorite person. I know you and I got some bad history because of Kira, but shawty, that was just business; never was it personal. Your folks owed me some bread and I wanted it. I hope you ain't got no hard feelings over that shit. Besides that was over a year ago."

I stared at him while he attempted to be civil. I couldn't believe he was so casual about the situation. I decided to let it go and see what he could do for me. If he wasn't stacking major figures then there was no need for us to even talk. The only way for me to find out if he was going to be my new sponsor was to play nice and see how much money he was willing to spend.

"Marshall, if we're gonna be friends then please don't call me Samantha. Everyone calls me Powder. That shit that happened with me and Kira is the past. I ain't worried about that and you shouldn't be either." I flashed him a warm and sexy smile.

Marshall returned the smile; we exited the car and joined Nee Nee and Rasaun. They were already inside the restaurant waiting to be seated by the hostess.

"I'm glad the two of you seem to be getting along." Nee Nee smiled.

Marshall took my hand in his and gave me a knowing nod.

"Yeah, Nee Nee, me and Powder are gonna be just fine," Marshall said.

The evening seemed to be going fine. I learned from the conversation that Marshall and Rasaun had during dinner that they were handling their street business together. They were careful not to speak on any amounts or say how much money they were getting in the streets. That didn't stop me from trying to guess how much money Marshall had. I didn't know shit about the street value of drugs, so the stuff they were talking about was beyond me. Anything they talked about I stored in my mental data bank to ask Shaunie about later. I had more than enough questions for her once we were alone. Like, why she didn't tell me I would be going out with Kira's ex-man. Something about going out with him had me feeling weird.

I know Kira was long gone, and she and Marshall no longer were an item, but something nagged and tugged at me telling me that this was more than a casual meeting. This was more than chance. I let it go and attempted to enjoy the rest of the evening.

When the date was over and they dropped me off, Marshall insisted on walking me to my door. I wasn't gonna stop him either. It wasn't like he didn't know what my situation with my parents was like. He had past dealings with my parents and their drug addiction.

So there wasn't shit to hide. He knew the ugly truth already, and he played a major part in my parent's downward spiral from their drug abuse.

"Powder, I enjoyed ya' company, shawty. When can I see you again?" Marshall asked.

My heart thumped a little faster at the thoughts of getting with him. Maybe I would get out of my parent's home after all and even sooner than I thought. The wheels of my mind started to turn.

"Why don't you call me and we can discuss all that." I responded, silently hoping that my phone stayed on long enough to receive the call.

Marshall reached in his pocket and pulled out his cell to lock my number in.

"I hope you call me sooner, rather than later shawty. Don't keep me waiting. I ain't about waiting around." He flashed me a million-dollar smile.

I took the opportunity to see what this nigga was really about. It was now or never because I wasn't gonna waste my time if his ass wasn't willing to donate to the causes that were most important to me, such as my shoes, clothes, and another place to live. There was no point in stalling and doing the whole dating thing if he wasn't going to give me the things I needed to survive.

"Marshall, I want to call you, but my phone might be off in a day or so. I just lost my gig I was working so I ain't sure how I'm gonna come up with the money to pay the bill," I said, pouting my full pink lips like an innocent child.

I watched him closely, waiting for him to react to

what I said. If he responded wrong then he would be waiting on a call that would never come. I didn't have time to waste on a broke-ass nigga that had nothing to offer but a stiff dick. I had learned many lessons well hanging around Nee Nee—and making sure I didn't waste my time fucking around with a man who wouldn't, or couldn't, spend dough on me like he should, was a valuable lesson learned!

I was pleasantly surprised that Marshall's facial expression never changed. He simply reached in his pocket and pulled out a knot of cash that was held together by a gold money clip. He pulled off several bills and handed them to me.

"Like I said, don't keep a nigga waiting. When I call, make sure you answer...so pay ya' phone bill or whatever you need to do to make sure you can stay up with me," he said with a smirk.

I gripped the fresh, crisp bills in my palm as if he was going to snatch them back. I nodded my head to let him know I had heard him, and then I turned to walk in my front door. Before I could get inside, Marshall slapped me across the ass. I didn't object; as a matter of fact, his gesture, no matter how rude, let me know he wanted something from me and I was going to give him whatever he needed as long as he kept my pockets laced.

As I entered the house, I smiled at the thought of getting more money from Marshall. I passed by my parents who were in the living room nodding in their usual spot. I turned up my nose and tucked the crisp bills inside my bra. Had either one of their junkie asses seen the dough I had gotten from Marshall, they would have been all over my ass trying to get a cut. I crept to my room like a thief in the night. Why I was creeping, I don't know, because neither one of them were sober enough to even notice that I had even come in the house. The thought of them getting high made me pick up my pace; I started to panic. *Where the fuck did they get the money to get their shit?* I thought as I raced to my room. Once inside my room, I found out where they had gotten the money from. My room was in an uproar. My belongings were thrown to and fro. I hurried over to my closet where I kept my chest. Only when I saw that my chest had not been opened was I able to breathe. I was getting real tired of my parents and their shit. In the end, they hadn't taken much. They had only taken a few pieces of costume jewelry and an old cell phone that didn't work anyway.

I flopped across my bed and wondered how the hell I was going to get out of the life I lived. I knew there was so much more out there for me. I just had to find out how to get it.

WWW.GSTREETCHRONICLES.COM

CHAPTER FOUR

The Truth Hurts

"**D**amn, that nigga might as well put a leash around your neck and stroll with you like a god damn puppy!" Nee Nee said sarcastically.

She and I were out getting our nails done. It was a beautiful Saturday and I ain't have a care in the world, except how much of Marshall's money I was going to spend. He was ringing my phone damn near to off the hook. I couldn't answer it because my nails were wet and I wasn't fucking up my design trying to answer a call I knew the outcome of. Marshall ain't want shit but to know where I was at all times. I told him many times before that he should have installed a Lo-Jack on my ass if he was so worried about where I was.

Life for me was on the up and up since I started fucking with Marshall. After the day he laced my pockets with the cash to pay my cell phone bill, we had been inseparable. Marshall was everything a bitch was looking for in a nigga. He kept me fly, and I didn't want for anything. The only downfall to dating Marshall was his temper, and his uncontrollable urge to fuck anything moving. We have been fucking with each other for the past seven months and I cannot count how many times I have busted his ass cheating on me with some broad. I have ended up in more fights than I care to remember, and locked up more times than I should have been for fighting him or whichever bitch I caught him with.

Regardless of all of Marshall's drama, I stayed right there. I had moved in with him and had no intentions on leaving him until I was good and ready. Needless to say, I wasn't ready. I was doing shit different this time. I was stacking the money Marshall was giving me. If anything happened to his ass, I was not going to be caught with nothing this time. I was going to have something put away just in case Marshall fell off, got knocked, or fucked around and got killed...or if I was simply sick of his cheating ass.

"You need to check his ass! It is always the guilty ones that do all of that insecure shit," Nee Nee said while blowing on her wet fingers.

I waved her off because there was nothing in this world that would make me go back to what my life had been before Marshall. I put up with his lies and overbearing behavior in order to keep a place to lay my head and to keep money in my bank account. Don't get me wrong, Marshall got on my fucking nerves and his cheating was driving me up a wall.

As I started thinking of his cheating, I was reminded that it was time for me to take my medication that I had been prescribed to clear up the latest gifts Marshall had given me—a bacterial infection and Chlamydia.

With all of this shit, I was still reluctant to leave his ass alone. Anything is better than living in the hood with your heroin-addicted parents, who would sell your dirty underwear off of your ass just to get high. I would deal with whatever I had to in order to make sure I never had to return to the piece of life I had before Marshall.

He could fuck whomever he wanted. He could call my cell phone all damn day and he could fuss about my whereabouts all he liked. That shit didn't faze me one bit; as long as he was paying, I was staying!

"Are we still going to Hell Razors to get our hair done?" Shaunie asked skipping over my nonchalant attitude about my boyfriend's behavior.

"Yeah. I have been thinking about dying my hair strawberry blonde. What do you think?" I asked waiting for Nee Nee to give me her opinion.

"I think you should. That shit is gonna be hot. That brown shit is tired anyway. You need a new look. You damn sure got the body! Now all you need is a new hairdo," she suggested.

We finished up our nails, headed a few doors down to Hell Razors, and joined in the weekend antics with the other females in the neighborhood. Some of them had changed their attitude about me and others still didn't fuck with me. I could care less just as long as those thirsty bitches knew I had arrived!

Hell Razors was the spot to be on a Saturday. You could find out all the gossip and get your shit done proper. On more than one occasion, shit had popped off while we were there getting our hair done. I had to admit, I enjoyed being in the thick of all the action. Only real bitches that dated niggas with money flocked to the shop to get their hair done. You had to either be paid, or be dealing with a paid nigga in order to afford the steep prices of the stylists who worked out of Hell Razors. Nee Nee and I sauntered into the shop and requested our normal stylists. After finding out that they would be free soon, we took a seat and listened in on all the neighborhood happenings. After waiting for an hour, and growing tired of my phone ringing nonstop with Marshall wanting to know where I was and when I would be home, it was finally my turn to be serviced.

My stylist, Bianca, who was also the shop's owner, sat me in her chair and started dishing out the latest gossip about who was fucking who. I swear that bitch knew more folks' business than Wendy Williams. One day someone was going to kick her ass for not minding her own damn business; and believe me, she had enough of her own shit going on. So much that she should have been dealing with why her baby daddy was fucking with her receptionist, Sasha. All of Bianca's business was in the streets, but she acted like she didn't know her man was fucking around. Maybe she just didn't care because he had paid for her salon.

"Powder, what are you gonna get done to this head today, boo?" Bianca asked, running her fingers through my scalp.

I thought about it for a few moments. I had never done anything to my hair other than added a few curls to my mousy brown locks. I was scared to death to do anything else to it, but it was time for a change.

"I want you to cut off a few inches and I want you to dye it blond," I stated, still unsure of what I was asking her to do.

Nee Nee looked over from the chair she was seated in and couldn't believe I was really about to have my hair chopped off and colored. I had talked about doing something drastic to my hair and appearance for a very long time, but I had never gotten up the nerve to really do it.

"Damn, bitch, it's about time you finally let me do something to this Katie Holmes, brown shit you been running around here with." Bianca laughed while she got to work on my head.

Bianca had been trying to convince me to dye my hair for the past several months. I sat in the chair listening to the happenings in the hood while I waited to see the end result of my decision to chop off and lighten my hair.

The gossip was more than amusing, it was downright entertaining. When Bianca handed me the mirror to see what she had done to my gold mane, I was shocked and pleased. It startled me at how a simple color change could change your attitude and appearance. Kim Kardashian ain't have shit on me.

Nee Nee was having her hair braided and was waiting to have the ends of her braids dipped in the boiling hot water to straighten them out, when the world's biggest hoodrat, Erica, strutted into the salon.

Erica had a bad reputation and she did not care

who knew she was a low down, dirty whore either. What made it so bad was that she wasn't a bad looking girl. She was actually pretty. She wore too much of everything though. Erica was the type who had to be seen so she would over-do everything to get attention. She would wear too much make-up, too little clothing and her weave was always tasteless. Her clothing choices reminded me of something a streetwalker would wear.

I suspected this bitch was the reason I had to pop these pills for the next five days to clear up this funky shit Marshall had given me. I had found her number in Marshall's phone and he couldn't explain why he had it. I had also discovered photos of her in his phone too. He tried to brush it off like every nigga' in the hood had pictures of Erica's ass. I wasn't stupid. Although she was a whore, and had probably sent those pictures to every nigga in the hood, I knew it was more to it than Marshall was making it out to be.

Just seeing her here made me want to smack the stupid grin she was wearing off of her Mary Kay clad face. I turned my nose up and turned my attention back to the conversation going on that was better than any television show.

Whenever I glanced in Erica's direction, she was staring right back at me. When she made eye contact with me, I swear I saw her roll her beady eyes at me. I could feel my temper rising and decided to be the bigger person and ignore her. She was nothing more than the side piece. I was *"that bitch"* on Marshall's arm; Erica and Marshall fucking around wasn't going to change that fact.

"Oooh Erica, that bag is hella' nice. Where did you get it?" Bianca cooed as she moved along the shop gathering supplies to start the quick weave she was about to put in Erica's hair.

"Oh, girl, this old thing?" Erica said holding up the new *Hermes'* bag that I knew cost well over five thousand dollars. I knew damn well that bag wasn't old because I had just received one just like it, in another color, from Marshall as a peace offering gift for him giving me a sexually transmitted disease.

I watched Erica closely because if she even made mention of my man, I could not be held responsible or accountable for what I would do to her.

Erica peered in my direction and said, "Bianca, you know my man Mars gives me whatever I want." She motioned towards the bling that was on her wrist.

My mind was screaming for me to get the fuck out of that salon and as far away as I could from Erica and the escalating situation. Instead, I sat there fuming. With the mention of Marshall's street name, Mars, Nee Nee turned her attention to me, only to see my cheeks turn bright red with humiliation and anger. Nee Nee's eyes then dropped to the identical *Hermes'* bag I had in my lap.

"You know he loves to spoil me and I love to show him how much I love to be spoiled." Erica gushed.

This dirty, diseased tramp was sitting there talking about the money my man had spent on her trifling ass in my face. I couldn't contain my anger, I jumped up and walked to where Nee Nee was seated having the rest of her hair finished.

"I am out of here. I will be in the store next door. Hit my phone when you are finished here. I need some fresh air. It just got foul as a motha' fucka in here," I said to Nee Nee, wrinkling my nose up as if something stunk. I couldn't get out of the door before Erica mumbled something under her breath. I didn't hear what she said as she was barely audible, but I knew that hoe was spitting venom in my direction and it was time for me to check that ass. Losing what little composure I had, I whirled around and stomped over to where she was sitting in the chair with a stupid grin plastered on her painted face.

"What did you say bitch?" I questioned her.

"I said fuck you, you skanky white bitch! I hope you do something about that stank pussy you're passing around..."

Before Erica could utter another word, I damn near broke my ankle grabbing up the boiling hot water that was being used to dip the tips of Nee Nee's braids, and I doused the hot liquid all over Erica's body. She howled out in pain and fell to the floor. She looked crazy the way she flopped around the floor trying to cure the burning sensation that had blanketed her body. My face twisted up in a sadistic smile. I dropped the container and commenced kicking and stomping her.

"I bet you won't be talking no more shit to me bitch! I better not catch you around my fucking man again or the next time I will kill you! That shit ain't a threat either, it's a fucking promise, hoe!" I screamed, still lifting my foot and connecting it with her chest and stomach over and over again.

I was going to show this bitch I wasn't soft and that she had fucked with the wrong one. I bent over and grabbed her up by the weave she was having removed, and tried my best to snatch that shit out of her head.

"Oh, my God! Powder, stop it! She has had enough. You are going to kill her in here!" Nee Nee screamed trying to pull me out of the salon.

I would not let go of Erica's tired ass weave. I dragged her along the floor as I was being pulled towards the doors of the salon by Nee Nee, who was trying desperately to get me to let go of Erica. There was no way this bitch was going to mess with my man, or my money, ever again without thinking twice about it. If she ever got up from the ass whooping I was putting on her, she was never going to forget this day.

"I am gonna call the cops on you, you crazy bitch!" Bianca screamed, rushing to the receptionist desk to call the police on me.

At the mention of the police, I finally let go of Erica and really assessed what I had really done. By dragging Erica around by her hair, we had managed to destroy the entire front of the salon. The booths were in an uproar and the patrons were all scrambling to get out of the way. I grabbed my bag off of the floor where I had dropped it, and grabbed up Erica's too. I crouched down next to where Erica lay and yanked the bracelet off of her wrist. There was no way she was going to keep walking around flossing the shit my man bought her like she was top flight. I made a beeline to the door with Nee Nee on my heels, and I fled from the salon as fast as I could before the cops came. We kept it moving swiftly to Nee Nee's car and hopped in, pulled off and got ghost as the police were swarming the salon to no doubt arrest my ass.

"Bitch, you are wild!" Nee Nee laughed nervously as she swerved in and out of traffic smoothly.

"I ain't wild. That bitch had it coming. Erica was a problem that needed to be solved. Case closed. Now take me home so I can deal with the other part of the equation. I ain't done dishing out the beat downs," I said, staring straight ahead.

I was pissed and I was not going to take this shit laying down either. Marshall was gonna have to answer for spending ends on that broke-down hoodrat. I could deal with the cheating to an extent, and his lying, but spending money on anyone other than me was more than I could take.

Never Get High On Your Own Supply

Nee Nee and I pulled up, a half an hour later, in front of the home I shared with Marshall and I had calmed down some. Once my adrenaline stopped pumping as hard as it had been, the fear of the police coming to cart my ass off to jail had set in. Sitting in Central Cell was not where I wanted to be over the weekend. None of the judges worked on the weekend, so if you got locked up over the weekend, you were stuck in a holding cell until Monday when they decided what to do with you.

"I hope the boys in blue don't come looking for your behind. Powder, you really shouldn't have done all of that to that girl. I understand why you did it, but throwing that hot water on her was uncalled for! I get that she deserved the ass whooping for flaunting what she was doing with Mars, but you went too damn far!" Nee Nee scolded me.

I rolled my eyes at her. All Nee Nee ever preached to me was for me to stand up for myself. Now, as soon as

I had done what she had been preaching for me to do, she was scolding me like I was a three-year-old child. I shook my head and ignored her comments. I tossed the bracelet, and the purse that was identical to my own, in my shopping bags and exited the car. I silently wondered whose side Nee Nee was really on.

"Do you want me to go inside with you? I don't need to be hearing anything about you throwing boiling water on Marshall. Are you gonna be aight, Powder?" Nee Nee asked me through the open window of the car.

"I am fine!" I said blandly taking notice of Marshall's car in the driveway.

I was glad his black ass was in the house because he was gonna hear my mouth about Erica. I chuckled to myself as I strutted up the walkway to our townhome thinking of the way Erica looked balled up on the floor trying to get away from my wrath. I thought about the beat down and the hot water I had thrown on Erica, and I knew she was going to be fucked up. There was no doubt in my mind I had done some damage with that scalding hot water. I bet she would think twice about trying to get out of pocket and step into a position that wasn't hers.

I wiped the smile off of my face before I entered the house. When I got inside, I could hear Marshall speaking to someone on the phone in the living room. I put down the bags I had and tip-toed to where I could hear the conversation better. He obviously didn't hear me come in.

"Look, baby, I am on my way. I will handle her once

I see her...you had no damn business flaunting our relationship around the shop like that in the first place. I ain't saying what Samantha did was right, but you have got to admit if it were you, you would have done the same shit. Tell Bianca thanks for giving me the heads up on what happened. Which hospital are you in?" Marshall said to the person on the other end of the phone.

There was no doubt in my mind it was Erica. When I heard him say, "hospital" I felt a smile creep to the corners of my mouth all over again. That bitch was lucky I hadn't killed her. She better take this shit as a lesson and stay out of my man's pockets and out of my fucking way, or there would be more than just hot water thrown on her dumb ass. And who the fuck was Bianca to call my man and tattletale on me?

I stood there listening to the conversation, not really moved by anything Marshall was kicking over the phone. I was used to his shit by now. He sucked his teeth in the manner that I hated so much, and it reminded me of a little girl throwing a tantrum.

"You let her take the bracelet and the purse? You let her get off on you like that?" He continued to question the caller.

Before he disconnected the call, I slipped into the living room and watched him squirm around. He must have known he had been caught because he didn't even bother to tell the caller "bye" before he hung up the phone.

I watched him closely to see what he was going to say about what had happened in the salon. I waited for him to check me like he had told the person he had been on the phone with. I played my position and never exposed my hand, never letting on that I had heard the entire conversation he had been having. Instead, I walked over to him with an evil smirk on my face.

Marshall looked at me full of curiosity. I pulled him into an embrace. From the way he squirmed, I could tell he was afraid of what I was going to do next.

"Hey, Daddy," I said purring into his ear, licking his earlobe as I whispered in his ear.

"I missed you today. I hope you missed me as much as I missed you. I was hoping we could spend some quality time together tonight," I said suggestively.

Marshall squirmed around uncomfortably. He had already promised that bitch, Erica, that he was on his way to be with her, and now I was deading all of that shit. What made matters worse was that I wasn't letting on that I had even had a confrontation with Erica. Marshall had the screw face on. I know he was waiting on me to go off about the fight I had with that bitch he was spending his money on.

"Can it wait until I get back? I had some shit come up that I need to handle like right now." Marshall pulled away from me.

I had him right where the fuck I wanted him. He thought he was a playa'. All along, he was getting played!

"Marshall, what is more important than me? What is more important than us?" I quizzed him. I was putting on a hell of an act. I could care less if that nigga went to be with that bitch. What he didn't know was that I wanted him to go to her, but it was gonna cost his ass to leave.

"You know ain't nothing more important than you baby girl. I just got some money to pick up," he lied through his teeth.

"Well, how about I go with you and then we can go out afterwards?" I pressed.

"You know I don't like you out there with me while I am making moves in the streets. That shit could get both of us locked up. I can't have my baby girl locked up now can I? Who would bail my ass out? Who would hold my shit down for me?" Marshall said trying to butter me up. He obviously didn't know there was no need to. I was already hip to his bullshit.

He must have thought shit was really *all good* because he seemed to relax a bit. Marshall was a fucking con artist to say the least, and it made me sick to my stomach. He was a manipulator just like my father. The only thing that cured the kind of sickness Marshall bestowed upon me was his money! Nothing more, nothing less!

"You know I always got you, Daddy. By the way, you didn't say anything about my hair." I cooed running my fingers through my freshly-colored hairdo.

"Damn, baby, you look like a million bucks for real now baby. Phat ass and all!" he said slapping me on my ass as I twirled around to show off my new cut and color.

I smirked at his statement. I knew he was trying to get away from me so he could go be with his bitch, Erica. I wanted nothing more than for him to go and see what damage I had done to his little bitch; but not before he fattened my pockets first. He had to pay for making me act like a fool in the hair salon. Now I was going to have to find somewhere else to get my hair done.

I snuggled up to him and batted my lashes, hoping he would become uncomfortable all over again so I could go in for the kill. I took his hand in mine and attempted to lead him to the second level of the home we shared.

Marshall pulled away from me.

"Powder, I got somewhere to go first and then we can play Kim K and Ray J when I come back; aight?"

"Damn, I never get to spend any time with you. Whenever I want to spend time with you, you blow me off. What's up with that shit, Mars? I mean, I did forgive you for the last shit you pulled. Most women wouldn't forgive their man for bringing them an STD." I pouted.

He walked over to the coffee table and took a seat on the over-priced couch. Marshall reached in his pocket and pulled out a knot of cash and a baggie. My eyes got big as saucers at the sight of the cash held together in the money clip. I knew I had his ass right where I wanted him. He was going to break me off with some money to get me off his ass so he could go and be with his bitch, Erica. He peeled several bills off of the stack and tossed them on the table along with a clear plastic bag which contained a powdery white substance which I knew was some kind of drug.

You never could tell what kind of drug Marshall was handling because he always had his hands in different street narcotics. Whatever you needed to get high, Marshall had on deck. He pulled a dollar bill from the folded stack of cash and rolled it into a tube. He proceeded to empty some of the powder on the glass table, then pushed it around with a card that was also clipped within the stack of bills until it was in a neat line. Marshall did the unthinkable in front of me and I could not believe my eyes. He snorted the entire line of what I had assumed was cocaine. My eyes almost bugged out of my head at the sight of him getting high. Sure, I smoked weed, but weed isn't a drug in my opinion.

Because of my parents' addiction, I vowed to never indulge in anything outside of smoking weed and drinking. I never wanted to become what they were—two strung-out hood junkies. Marshall knew I didn't condone drug use of any kind because of my parents.

"Marshall! What the fuck are you doing? I know damn well you ain't gonna sit there and get high in front of me! You know I don't even get down with shit like that! And just when did you start getting high off of that shit?" I questioned him in disgust.

"Damn, don't start with that nagging shit, Sam. I got to make some rounds and I need to get my head right before I hit the streets. I don't fuck with this shit all the time. I do it just to take the edge off sometimes," he said casually. He held one side of his nose and snorted again. He emptied more of the powder on the table and made two more lines. This time he extended his hand with the rolled up dollar in my direction.

I rolled my eyes at him in disbelief.

"You have got to be fucking kidding me! You're a fucking junkie!" I fussed.

Marshall hopped up from where he was sitting and

moved swiftly to where I was standing motionless. He grabbed me around my throat and backed me up against the wall.

"Bitch, you better watch your fucking mouth! I ain't no god damn junkie! You and I both know what junkies are, and I ain't one of 'em! Junkies are mother fucka's like your parents. Niggas like me are bosses, not junkies! Do you fucking understand me, bitch?" he slurred, throttling my neck.

I didn't know who this demon was. Marshall and I had had our fair share of fights and arguments, but this nigga had lost his mind shoveling that shit up his nose and coming for me like he was crazy. Shit had switched up. I just wanted him to let me go and get the fuck out. My plan to get money from his ass was backfiring. I was used to fighting with Marshall, but his strength was almost superhuman. I clutched at his hands, fighting against the two hundred, forty-five pounds that were crushing my windpipe.

"Mars, you are going to kill me! Please let me go!" I managed to gurgle.

And just like that, he let me go. It was as if someone had turned on a light switch. He was Mars again, and he stared at me blankly for a moment while I shivered in total fear of him. He turned around and walked over to the table where the cash and his coke had been thrown, snatched up his keys, and proceeded to head to the door. Before he could get out the door, he stopped, turned around and stared at me standing there breathlessly against the wall.

"Buy yourself something nice and I will see you when I get back." He gestured towards the money he had left on the table, along with the lines of cocaine he had left behind. "Oh, and clean that shit up too," he demanded, pointing at the white powdery substance.

Something about the way Marshall had turned his anger on and off was astonishing. It wasn't until he had let himself out the door that I dared to breathe. I didn't move until I heard his car engine crank up. This shit Marshall pulled was nothing like anything I had ever seen before. It was as if he was trying to kill me and then just like that he was himself again. I damn near ran snatching the bills up off of the table and went to the master bedroom to count the wad of cash I had almost died for.

I learned a very valuable lesson not to fuck with Marshall while he was tooting that shit up his nose, and it further showed me why I was never going to fuck around with anything stronger than weed.

A Different Kind Of High

I t was a sunny afternoon in the District, and I was not happy that I had to waste my time accompanying Marshall to meet up with his supplier, Adekite. Sure, I loved when Marshall was making the cash, but I hated when he and his business associates got together. Marshall had a fucked up way of making me feel out of place. I knew he would take me along because I was a diversion. I was like his personal police blocker. Whenever he would pick up large quantities of cocaine, he would have me ride with him in case the cops pulled him over. He knew that they would see nothing more than an inter-racial couple out for a ride, instead of what it really was—a nigga transporting narcotics over state lines.

The things Marshall used to do that I used to think were flattering were now sickening. He would show me off like I was a trophy, token white girl. This nigga must have thought he was Kanye West with the way he flaunted me around. I enjoyed the attention, but I hated that he made me feel like that was the only reason he kept me around.

I was so confused about our relationship. He would make me feel like his queen at times, and at others he would make me feel like a fool. Word on the street was that he was still fucking with Erica. Apparently her burns weren't severe enough to stop her from whoring around with my man. She had better stay out of my way if she knew what was good for her, because this time I would see to it that she was would be doing more than a few weeks in the hospital. I would cripple and disfigure that bitch for fucking with my man and my money.

Marshall was starting to get on my damn nerves! He was always creeping off and lying about his where-a-bouts. Not to mention, he was snorting that shit up his nose at an alarming rate now. I guess he hadn't heard the saying, "Never get high on your own supply." Either he had heard it and didn't care, or he really thought he didn't have a habit.

I was sitting there in Marshall's supplier's crib while Marshall sampled some of the product he was supposed to be moving through the city. I sat there bored with the whole thing. I had gotten used to Marshall tooting that shit up his nose now.

I admired the expensive paintings hanging on the walls and wondered how much money they had cost Adekite. They were all exotic and showed naked women of all colors engaged in some type of tribal dance. It seemed fitting for Adekite to have some weird shit like that around. He was a weirdo. Something about this meeting was different from all the other times we had met up with Adekite. Instead of Marshall becoming hyper and bouncing off the walls like he normally did when he was high, he seemed to slow down. His speech was slurred and it was if he were in slow motion. Adekite had always struck me as odd. He was from Nigeria and to say I was scared of him was an understatement. His lean, 6'4", 160 pound frame reminded me of the rapper Wiz Khalifa. There was something sinister behind his eyes. I hated being around him too long. There was an unnatural air about him, and it always made me feel uneasy that he never seemed to leave me until we were far away from him.

Marshall's head hit his chest and his eyes rolled up and back until nothing could be seen but the whites of them. It scared the shit out of me. I jumped up from where I was sitting and began to panic that Marshall was overdosing on whatever he had snorted up his nose. Running to his side, I shook him and tried to bring him out of the drug-induced haze he was succumbing to.

"Marshall...Marshall!" I screamed, grabbing at the fabric of his expensive Ralph Lauren collared shirt.

He was unresponsive and I was afraid he was dying. I had seen many junkies, including my parents, get sucked into the cold darkness of a drug. Something about this scene was eerily familiar. I had seen it before. This was beyond scary, and I wanted Marshall to snap out of it before he slipped into a place where he would not return to me.

"He is aight. Let him enjoy the high. I am sure it is

one he will never forget." Adekite laughed as I frantically tried to keep Marshall among the land of the living.

"It doesn't look like he is enjoying it," I said with my voice cracking.

I was no fan of Marshall's, but he was my only way to the life I felt I deserved; and if his ass died, I would be stuck starting over from scratch all over again and I was not interested in cozying up to another man. I didn't want to try to find another man to provide for me.

"Oh, believe me, he is in heaven, Samantha," Adekite said in his thick accent.

His laugh was so cold it sent shivers up my spine. I hated the way he said my name. I glared in Adekite's direction, hoping he could see the desperation in them. Instead, he stood there unmoved with a look of complete satisfaction and pleasure etched across his face.

"You look surprised to know that your man was so easily drugged and taken out of the game."

I stared at him confused at his statement.

"What do you mean taken out of the game? What did you give him?" I questioned Adckite but never once did I stop attempting to keep Marshall among the living.

"Samantha, you are a smart girl. I am quite sure you have known for some time that your man is a junkie. I just gave him what he was looking for. I gave him a high he would never forget. I gave him the one that will be with him forever. He will wake up needing and craving this high. If he doesn't satisfy the insatiable need to get high, he will get sick; just like heroin addicts do."

I let the collar of Marshall's shirt go and focused on

what Adekite was telling me.

"Why would you drug him up, especially if he moves weight for you? If he is a user then he will be no good to you!" I fussed, confused by Adekite's actions.

"Instead of wondering why I did it, you should be wondering what you are going to do now that he is a dope fiend.

I shook my head back and forth. This shit could not be happening. I could not wrap my mind around why Adekite had slipped Marshall heroin instead of giving him the cocaine we had come there to cop. My mind was in a million different places. I felt like I was ten years old again. I remember so vividly the first time I witnessed my mother and father shooting the same drug in their veins. I don't know how I couldn't recognize the type of high Marshall was riding.

Adekite got up from where he was seated and joined me next to Marshall, who was so gone off of the dope that he was drooling all over his shirt.

"You slipped him heroin, but why? Why would you do that to us?"

"Marshall has been stealing from me so long that he is lucky I don't kill him! I figure being a dope fiend is the worst punishment for a nigga who steals from me."

I was dumfounded, and above all, confused on what Marshall had stolen from Adekite.

"What did he steal? I am sure we can fix this!" I screamed, trying to get Adekite to show some sympathy for me.

"He stole my product and has not paid for it. I simply

waved a sample under his nose as I always have. I noticed the last few times Marshall has come here to re-up, he has been way too eager to sample my product. He has been coming with short money, and that's what this all boils down to—my money. I looked at Marshall as a brother; but when I saw he had an addictive personality, I started thinking that our business together was over. Samantha, a boss never gets high off of the shit he is supposed to be peddling to these fools on the street. Your man got caught." Adekite smiled a wicked smile.

I panicked. I knew once Marshall came down off of his high, shit was never going to be the same. I thought about having to go back home, or even worse, not having anywhere to go at all. I knew if I asked Nee Nee could I crash with her, she would let me, but it would be short lived. Nee Nee didn't like anyone around her man for too long. I could understand. If he was my nigga, I would act the same way.

My mind was all over the place. I knew I had some paper stashed away, but not enough to pay the bills, the mortgage on our townhome, the car notes and the other expenses we had acquired. My mind was moving in fast forward. With Marshall's recreational drug use, turned habit, I am sure he didn't have too much put away either. He was getting high far more than he was in the streets.

I turned my attention back to Adekite. He was my only hope. I stared deep into his eyes trying to find an ounce of sympathy and found none. I still swallowed my pride and went at him the only way I knew how.

"Adekite, surely you know I didn't have anything

to do with this shit. I didn't even know he was using like this." I lied. I looked away from the piece of trash nodding in the chair and back to the man who could make or break my entire life, Adekite.

"So, what am I supposed to do? You turned him into a damn fiend. He is never gonna be able to stay sober long enough to make your money for you without getting sick." I whined.

My whining had no effect on Adekite. A sly smile formed across his face.

"Samantha, get my money and I will make sure you are taken care of. If you get my money back to me in a timely manner, I may even have a position for you to play; but for now, get your junkie ass boyfriend the fuck up out of here!" The smile had disappeared from his face and was replaced with a scowl that made my heart feel like it was going to stop.

My fear was instantly replaced with anger. I didn't have too many choices in the matter. I was going to have to ride this out with Marshall, and hope he could shake the effects of the drug he was force fed until I could come up with another plan or get Adekite his money.

I tried to get Marshall up so we could get the fuck out of Adekite's sight before he took our chances at freedom and our lives back. He could easily change his mind and decide to kill us instead of punishing Marshall by turning him out.

"I will get someone to get him out of here," Adekite said, pressing the intercom and speaking a language I could not understand.

Under a minute later, two hulking figures appeared at the doorway. Adekite nodded in Marshall's direction. The two goons grabbed him up under his arms and carried him out of Adekite's office. I followed behind them with my head down.

"Samantha. Get my money or the same thing can happen to you!" Adekite threatened.

I shivered, left his office and out the front door. I got to the car and Marshall was already inside in the passenger seat. He was leaning so far forward his head was resting on the dashboard. I slid into the driver's side and took a look at Marshall.

"You ain't worth it nigga! You ain't worth it at all." I mumbled. I cranked up the car and pulled off before Adekite sent his goons after us. I couldn't help but to have mixed feelings about all of it though. It served Marshall's scandalous ass right. All the shit he had done to me in the very recent past was catching up to him. I was afraid his demons were going to be gunning for me too.

In The Jungle, The Mighty Jungle

"Has Rasaun ever mentioned anything about Marshall?" I asked Nee Nee.

We were having lunch on the waterfront of Proud Mary's in Fort Washington, Maryland. I wasn't there to really have a social outing with my only friend. I was there to find out what she knew about Marshall.

He had done just what I knew he would. He had become addicted to the powerful drug and he was becoming a shell of himself. I didn't know what to do with him. Adekite had totally cut him out of the game and money was funny to say the least. I had resorted to selling Marshall's stuff just to put gas in the car. Shit was wicked and I couldn't just walk away. Where was I going to go? I couldn't go to my parents. Hell, I didn't even know if those no good motha' fucka's were dead or alive, and for real...I ain't give a fuck.

I had sold just about everything that I could bare to part with. What I hadn't sold, Marshall went behind my back and sold to get high.

"What do you mean, 'mention anything'?" Nee Nee asked, raising her eyebrow in curiosity.

I sat quietly trying to figure out how I was going to find out what everyone else knew without letting our dark secret out. I had been trying my best to cover for Marshall's absence over the last few weeks. If he had business to handle, I did that shit myself. I told Marshall's clients that he had sent me in his place to make all of his transactions. I told them that it looked better with me doing the hand-to-hand shit because no one would suspect me of selling drugs.

My plan had worked and none of Marshall's folks knew what the fuck was going on. I had made almost all of the money Marshall owed Adekite. I was only a few grand short, and the way things were moving along, I was sure to get it. At times, I wanted to take the money I had been hustling up and hit the ground running. Every dime I made pushing the last little bit of Marshall's weight went to paying Adekite back the money Marshall owed him. I didn't need the head of a Nigerian drug ring on my ass for some shit I didn't have anything to do with. Instead, I sold what I could to survive, and paid Adekite, little by little, and now that number was getting smaller.

I shifted my thoughts back to my own little investigation. I needed to know what the streets were saying about my dried-up, dope fiend of a man. I was embarrassed as hell that I was associated with him.

Shaunie waved her hand in front of my face, attempting to get my attention. I had drifted off into my own thoughts.

"Hello! What do you mean, 'mention anything'?" Nee Nee repeated, taking a bite of her steak that I wished I could afford to enjoy.

"I was wondering if anyone had noticed I was handling all of Marshall's street business," I said, pausing to read Nee Nee's face.

"What the hell is your paranoid ass talking about, Powder? Ain't nobody in the streets checking for you like that. They are checking for me though!" she giggled.

I was glad to hear no one was on to me pushing weight to pay off a debt. I didn't need them nosey mother fucka's in my business. It was either give them more shit to talk about, or have someone trying to run up on me and rob my ass.

I didn't give a fuck about what niggas thought about Marshall because as soon as I got my ass in the clear with Adekite, I was gonna drop Marshall's ass like a bad habit, and see about how I was going to come up on my own. This living off of a nigga was far more trouble than it was worth.

Nee Nee and I had wrapped up our lunch and I hustled along to meet Adekite. I had more ends to get to him and I had every intention of getting them to him. I made my way through the city until the streets gave way to the immaculate homes of the suburbs of Montgomery County Maryland.

I drove along thinking about how I deserved to be living out *among* the wealthy movers and shakers. Don't get me wrong, Marshall and I used to live swell just a few short months ago, but since his dumb ass went and got caught slipping, our home is now damn near empty. His ass doesn't even leave the house unless he is going to find a way to get high.

Looking in Marshall's face lately has started to make me sick! Living with him has become difficult and he doesn't even see the problem. He really doesn't believe he has an addiction. He keeps singing the same song about how he can kick the habit if he wants too!

This stupid mutha' fucka' had the nerve to ask me if I wanted to try that shit with him. I know he is a dope fiend to the max because he went as far as trying to sneak out of the house a few nights back with the last little bit of product that I had to move. He had the nerve to have stuffed it in one of my designer bags and sneak it out the door to sell. When I caught him, I wanted to beat him down for taking the little bit of my belongings I had left that were of value. I had to threaten his life if he didn't give me my shit.

The worst part of it all is the fact that he is always home, unless he is out trying to find a way to get high. I guess he and his lil' hoe, Erica, must have gone their separate ways, or else she decided she couldn't fuck with him since he was down and out and his money was funny. Maybe the bitch knew he was strung out and didn't want to have no parts of the drama that came along with him now. No matter what it was, Marshall had been right in the house, high as hell and getting on my fucking nerves begging me for money he knew I didn't have.

I suggested that he go to rehab and try to get some help because he obviously had a problem. Then he gives me the same song and dance that everything will be ok. He keeps swearing day, in and day out, that he is gonna quit. I guess he forgot that because of my parents, I knew about this shit before I even got with him. No matter how they got their high, they were addicted; and once that drug got a hold of you, there was no shaking it!

If this nigga keeps playing around and refusing help, I am gonna have to take matters into my own hands. The last time I made a drop off at Adekite's, he told me to prove to him that I can hold shit down and he will help me out. I think it is time for him to help! I am keeping my end of the bargain and have proved myself worthy. I am getting sick of Marshall and I had been thinking of ways to get rid of him.

My mind wandered further into my problems until I pulled up in front of Adekite's home. I pulled into the driveway and killed the engine. I grabbed my purse from the passenger side seat and exited the car. I may have looked like I had it all together the way I strutted up the walkway, however, I was dying on the inside. I knew that it was all a show because my life was fucked up from my point of view.

I rang the bell and Katavious, Adekite's brother, answered the door and quickly ushered me into the front room after patting me down. I hated that I had to go through this shit every time I came here to see Adekite. One of his goons, or his brother's violated my space every time I came. I knew they were doing their jobs, but they would go through my purse and riffle through my things and it made me feel uncomfortable.

Adekite's brother, Katavious, had a chip on his shoulder and made it very obvious that he didn't like me around. The feeling was mutual; I didn't like his ass either!

His brother, Ohruh, was different. He seemed sweet and innocent. He didn't seem as though he belonged in this type of life. Something about his eyes told me that he wasn't built for this, but he didn't have a choice. His brothers had forced his hand.

Katavious led me to the study where Adekite was seated on the couch watching soccer on the flat screen. He barely acknowledged that we had come into the room.

"Aye, Adekite your snow bunny is here," Katavious said, shaking his head. His disapproval of me being in his presence was apparent. I could feel the blood rushing to my face from embarrassment. I knew I was white, they knew I was white, but why did everyone always have to point that shit out like I ain't know.

Adekite looked away from the TV and motioned for me to come take a seat next to him. I sat in the same spot where Marshall had been marked for death. Adekite waved his brother out of the room.

Katavious's eyes grew dark and cold.

"I know you ain't gonna dismiss me like I ain't shit in front of this bitch!" he spat in his heavy accent.

Adekite turned his attention back to the television as if he hadn't heard what his brother had said to him. He wore a look of amusement on his face at a commercial that played on the giant screen and paid Katavious no mind.

Katavious said something in his native tongue. He gave me one last look and left the room. I sat there in complete silence. I was uncomfortable every time I had to come here. I always wondered if Adekite was going to make an example of me like he had done Marshall, so that always made me uneasy.

At any time Adekite could do away with me, and I knew it. He finally turned the television off and focused his attention on me.

"You got something for me?" he asked. His eyes bore into me like daggers.

I nodded and shuffled through my purse for the envelop that contained the cash I had come to drop off. I handed him the manila envelope that was stuffed with money and waited in silence while he peeked inside. I could tell he barely counted it before tossing it on the table where he had his feet propped up.

Adekite turned the television back on and began flipping through the channels. I took that as my queue to leave. He obviously didn't want to be bothered unless it had something to do with his money and that was something I didn't have all of, so I stood to make my exit. I didn't have the nerve to ask him about helping me deal with Marshall and his problem. I felt like a fucking fool for even thinking he would really help me. I mean really...why would he? He was the reason my shit was falling apart anyway.

I had made my way to the door when Adekite called

me back to him.

"I didn't tell you, you could leave. Sit down!" he barked, his menacing eyes pierced me. I felt as though he were looking through me instead of at me. I quickly took a seat and I instantly became very aware of where I was and what I was doing. This man had the power to make me disappear, and at the rate I was going, no one would even miss me besides Nee Nee.

"You leave when I let you leave. You understand?" Adekite said, clearly angry with me trying to leave without him dismissing me.

I dropped my head afraid to look at him. His stare was cold and intimidating.

"We still have business," he said, turning his attention back to the television and I was grateful; because I hated the way he looked at me.

"The last time we spoke I made you a promise; did I not?"

I looked up at him almost relieved that he seemed to remember the help he offered me.

"Yes...yes you did. I just thought you were busy or maybe you had forgotten. I didn't want to be a bother," I said, stumbling over my words. I finally shut up so I wouldn't sound like a fool and he change his mind and decide not to help me with Marshall.

"How is Marshall?" Adekite chuckled, still staring at the huge television.

I wrinkled my nose up.

That's a dumb fucking question! You know damn well he is a fucking zombie and it's all your damn fault! I thought to myself. I dare not say that shit out loud. I was scared to death thinking of what he might do to me.

"He's aight." I lied. But I knew he already knew the truth. He had been peddling heroin long enough to know that anyone who was strung out on that shit was far from okay. He laughed a hearty laugh that made the hair on the back of my neck stand to attention and I could feel the beads of sweat forming on my forehead. Being around him was enough to drive anyone crazy.

"That nigga is far from aight. If my suspicions are correct, he is fucked up; is he not?" Adekite asked, finally looking at me. I knew he was doing it to see if he could read my face. He wanted to see if I was lying to him and I immediately regretted that I had.

I shook my head.

"Look, Samantha, I don't have time to play games with you. If I ask you something, you are to answer me honestly. If you don't, all bets are off."

He got up from the couch and walked over to the huge desk that sat in the corner and went inside. He pulled out a syringe and held it up. I was deathly afraid of what he was going to do with it. After all, this is the man that had turned my boyfriend into a junkie. I didn't put anything past him. He crossed the room again and handed the syringe to me. I didn't take it immediately; afraid that he was up to something. Adekite could see my hesitation and a huge grin appeared on his face. It looked as foreign as his accent sounded.

"I know you don't trust me Snow Bunny, but you and I are one in the same. I see you. You are thirsty. You're hungry. You are like a mighty lion in the jungle and you will kill your own cubs to get what you want. I see you," he repeated. He put the syringe down on the table.

I watched him intently now. I was intrigued. I wanted to know how he felt that he and I were the same. He was a drug dealing murder. I just wanted the finer things in life. There were no similarities, none whatsoever. I was more like the cub he spoke about. I was soft and needed to be taken care of. Adekite was a beast and I was being nice describing him as such.

Again, he sat there reading my thoughts. "I bet you are wondering why I say we are alike? Think about it Samantha, you want what you want, when you want it. I am willing to bet you will take it, if you had too. You would kill for the things you want. I too would kill for what I want. I am not beyond taking what I want if it were to bring me the satisfaction of having the finer things," Adekite said. His eyes were locked on mine now.

I had to admit he had piqued my curiosity.

"Samantha, you and I are one in the same. I will kill for mine. The question is will you?"

Adekite picked up the syringe and this time I didn't avoid taking it from his hands. I examined the syringe and I could clearly see there was a milky-like fluid in it. As I examined the needle, Adekite spoke up again. "Go to him. Give *it* to him. Then come to me. Do not come to me if you cannot handle what needs to be done. Do you understand?"

I slid the needle into my purse and nodded my head,

letting Adekite know I fully understood what he wanted me to do. I had come to him for help and he was giving me a way to get out of this messy shit with Marshall. I understood fully what he was doing. He was once again making me prove myself. He was giving me a way out without having to get his hands dirty, and for the first time since I had ever been in Adekite's presence, I smiled. It was cold and it matched the one plastered across his face and something inside me felt familiar. I knew that feeling. It was that same feeling I had the day I had beat the hell out of Kira. It was the same feeling I had when I doused Erica with the boiling water. It was revenge; and it felt oh, so sweet!

G Street Chronicles /   69

CHAPTER EIGHT

Lights...Death...Police...Action.

I pulled up in front of the townhouse I shared with Marshall after leaving Adekite's. I sat in the car for thirty minutes pondering what I was about to do. As different as Adekite and I were looks and background wise, he had spoken nothing but the truth about my hunger. He was right. I wanted the finer things in life. I deserved them and I had to figure out how I was going to get them, even if that meant taking them by force.

I got out of the car, walked into the house, and sat my purse down on the counter. I decided against prolonging what I needed to do to be the queen of my jungle. It was time for Marshall to go, and he was going to go right now so I could go about the business of ruling my life as I saw fit. There was no room in the kingdom for a junkie. Marshall had to go. He was causing more problems than he was worth. His addiction was driving me insane as though it were mine.

I rummaged through my purse and pulled out the syringe which was filled with what I knew was a hot dose. All I had was one chance to get this right and if I fucked up, I could wind up in jail or dead. I could not fuck this up. I put on my game face and called out to Marshall who was no doubt in the house. *Where else would he be?*

"Marshall, baby, I am home. Where are you?" I called out trying not to sound like I was up to something. I could hear him stumbling around on the second level of our once lavish home, and I made my way up the steps in the direction of the sounds. I chuckled thinking about how Adekite had said I was a lion. If only he knew I was as meek as a church mouse.

My heart drummed in my chest. By the time I had reached the top landing, I was so scared I almost turned around and said *fuck it*! Deep down, I knew I didn't have to do this shit. I could take the syringe and empty it into the toilet in the bathroom that was just to my left and never think about what I had contemplated again.

My greed and desire to have more got the better of me and I inched closer to the master bedroom where I could hear Marshall moaning and bumping around.

The combination of the thundering in my chest and the bumping sound coming from the room almost drove me insane. When I reached the doorway of the bedroom I shared with my drug dealer turned junkie boyfriend, I almost threw up from the smell that hung thick in the air. The smell of bile and shit made me gag. There was no doubt that Marshall had not had his fix and it was causing him to be sick. I held my breath and walked across the threshold as calmly as I could. At first

I didn't see Marshall until I walked over to his side of the bed. Again, I almost turned around and ran away from the madness.

Marshall was balled up on the floor; wedged between the nightstand and the bed. He was covered in sweat and his clothes were soiled with shit and vomit. He was banging his head on the floor trying to make the sickness that had taken control of his bodily functions subside. He was moaning over and over. The sound of a grown man falling apart was enough to make me want to drive a knife through my eardrums, just so I didn't have to hear him anymore.

It took Marshall a moment to notice I was standing there. When he did, his sunken eyes seemed to glimmer with a little bit of hope. There was no doubt in my mind that he thought I had come to save him from the sickness that was taking over him. He had no idea I was there to do just that. I was going to make it all go away.

"Powder! Where you been? I have been waiting on you all damn day, baby. You got a few dollars to help me out? I'm real sick baby and I swear this will be the last time. I just need this to get well enough to get myself out of here to get some help." Marshall lied.

I didn't say anything. I stared at this pathetic piece of shit and couldn't help but wonder what made me want him in the first place. Then it clicked. My greed made me want him. My need to be on top made me deal with him.

Marshall sat up and continued begging me for money I didn't have, and watching him be so weak made it easier for me to do what I had come home to do. I took a deep breath through my mouth and walked over to him.

"Come on, Daddy. I got something for you," I said.

Marshall's eyes lit up like a kid on Christmas Day. He started babbling and grunting the closer I got to him. The stench coming off of his body made me want to turn around and run. My lungs were screaming for fresh air. Still, I inched closer to him. When I was close enough, Marshall stuck his greedy hand out for me to hand him whatever it was he thought I was going to give him. With one swift motion I had popped the cap off of the laced syringe and lunged at him. I jabbed the syringe in the side of his neck.

"Yeah, you bitch ass nigga! I got something for that ass now!" I cried out feeling victorious.

I felt like everything Adekite said I was. I felt mighty, like the queen of my jungle.

Marshall seemed unmoved by the syringe that was hanging out of the side of his neck. His eyes fluttered closed as I had seen them do on many occasions before when his high caused him to drift away into his drug-induced haze. I stood there wondering had Adekite bamboozled me until Marshall's eyes sprung open and he began twitching wildly. He batted at the needle that was still hanging from his neck. Frothy foam formed at the corners of his mouth and he started to cough and vomit. I jumped out of the way before he threw up on me.

"Powder! Powder, it burns! Oh, my god, it burns!

Make it stop!" He whimpered, clutching at the empty syringe. He pulled himself up off of the floor, using the bed as a crutch, and his bowels let loose. He was finally able to pull the now empty needle from his neck. The vein in the middle of his forehead pulsated and twitched. Marshall reached out for me. I took two steps back and watched in amazement. His thrashing about reminded me of a center ring act at the circus. His body twisted into positions the human body should not be in.

"What did you do to me, bitch? I'm gonna kill you!"

Marshall fell back into his own bodily fluids. His chest heaved up and down as he called me all kinds of names and threatened my life.

I laughed at his threats that meant nothing to me. "I'll see you in hell mother fucka'! You did this shit to yourself! You ain't shit, but a junkie!" I snorted between laughs.

I don't know why the whole scene seemed so funny to me, but it was amusing.

Marshall made one last attempt at saving himself by reaching for the phone that was on the nightstand. Watching him try to save his life caused me to laugh harder. Under normal circumstances, one would have been afraid of him attempting to call the police. Instead, I wanted him to. Really, who were they going to believe, me or him. He was the drug dealer turned junkie, and I was the white woman who had never done anything to get in trouble; or at least nothing I had been caught for.

In Marshall's frantic attempt to save himself, he turned the nightstand over on top of him and finally all his thrashing about ceased.

I took a deep breath before moving closer. I put two fingers on his neck to see if I could feel a pulse and when there was none, the smile I already wore widened. I took the phone from his hand and dialed 911. I put on the best performance of my life when the operator came on the line.

"911. What's your emergency?"

"Come quick! I think my boyfriend...overdosed!" I sniffled.

I rattled off the address to the dispatcher and slammed the phone down, snatched up the needle, found the discarded top, and dropped them into an old shoe box.

I didn't give a fuck if they found that shit or not. They would think it was his too and all the drugs that were already coursing through Marshall's system were enough to label this an accidental overdose. I was confident of it!

I was pacing around the room trying to make sure I had my lie straight before the police got there, when I caught a glimpse of myself in the mirror and paused. I forgot all about the smell in the room and Marshall's dead body. I smiled at my reflection. Something about me was a little off, but I liked it. I wondered if Adekite had seen it. Maybe he could see me for who I really was. Maybe I really did have the heart for this shit.

Before I could get wrapped up in my thoughts of how I could use this situation as a stepping stone, I heard banging on the front door. I ran down the steps and swung the door wide open. The first officer who walked inside gave me a once over and I glared at her. She looked at me accusingly. The bitch didn't even speak.

What the fuck is this bitch looking at? I hope she ain't trying to size me up. The bitch just got here and she is already looking at me funny. I thought.

I figured I had better act like my boyfriend was lying dead in our bedroom instead of fucking around with this fed. I softened up my face and started to act the part of a woman who had just lost her boyfriend.

"He's upstairs!" I said breathlessly to the second officer who entered in behind his partner. He was tall, dark and handsome. My heart skipped a beat when my eyes locked in on him. I could tell there was an obvious attraction between us.

"Ma'am, what's going on? We got a call from this residence about a possible overdose. The paramedics are on the way. Where is the victim?" The female cop asked, interrupting my inspection of her partner who had my full attention. I turned my attention to the female cop, and then pointed to the stairs. She started making her way to the stairs and noticed her partner hadn't moved to follow her.

"Officer Kern, will you be accompanying me to see what's going on, or are you going to stay down here?" she said smartly.

She was obviously annoyed with the spark that was growing between me and her partner.

Officer Kern joined his partner and they made their way up the stairs. I didn't know if I should follow them, make a run for it out the front door, or stay put. I figured if I ran, they would just go through my shit and find out who I was and track my ass down in the streets. I wouldn't have been able to go far. It wasn't like I could just drive off and they would never catch me. My shit was all over the place in the house. If I wanted to look like I ain't have shit to do with this shit, I had better stay my ass right there.

After a few moments of standing there, I decided I had to know what they were up there doing. I hated to go back up there, but I just had to know what was going on. Once I got to the top of the steps, I could hear the female officer making a call over the radio. She was making the call to have the coroners make their way to the house.

After she was done calling for the coroners and the detectives, I heard that bitch whisper to her partner. I tiptoed a little closer to the doorway so I could hear just what she was saying.

"What do you really think happened here? Do you think she had something to do with this? Maybe we should question her to see what she will tell us." The female officer urged her male counterpart.

I didn't give him a chance to respond to her nosey ass before I stepped in the doorway, boldly making my presence known. I wanted that stupid bitch to know I had heard every fucking word she had said about me. When she saw me standing there, she knew she was busted. The handsome Officer Kern didn't seem to notice any of the tension between me and his bitch of a partner.

"Ma'am, you really shouldn't be up here. If you don't

mind, we need you to wait down stairs and we will be down in a second to talk to you," Officer Kern said sympathetically.

I nodded at him. I wanted to spit on that nosey whore who stood there looking at me accusingly. Instead, I went back down the steps and took a seat in at the kitchen table and waited until Officer Kern and his partner had come back downstairs. Once they came back down the stairs, the female officer went outside to write up some information and wait on the coroner and the crime scene detectives to arrive.

Officer Kern joined me at the kitchen table and took a seat across from me. As he spoke, I studied his chestnut-colored skin, and his chocolate brown eyes. He was so fine I had to stop myself from asking him a few questions of my own. This man was so fucking hot I wanted him to interrogate me by force if necessary. The whole time he spoke to me, I watched his lips, wondering what they would feel like on my skin. Something about killing Marshall and this man was turning me on. It was the craziest thing I had ever felt. It seemed like it would be taboo for the officer to take me in the kitchen of my deceased ex's home after I had put that nigga out of his misery.

"Ma'am, are you ok?" Officer Kern asked, snapping me out of my crazy thoughts.

"Yes. I'm...I'm ok. I think the shock of all of this is getting to me. I can't believe he is really gone. I told Marshall he needed to get some help. He promised me he was gonna stop using." I cried, hoping to gain the officer's trust since it was very clear his partner didn't trust me at all. I needed this man on my side if I wanted to get out of this shit with my freedom. It would be a bonus if I could see him again too.

"You never told me your name, ma'am," Officer Kern said.

"My name is Samantha. Samantha Underwood. But everyone calls me Powder." I sniffled through fake tears.

Officer Kern slid a card across the table. "If you need to talk, I'm here. I hope I'm not out of line, but I would like to help you through this if you need someone. This can't be easy and I can't imagine what you're going through," he said compassionately.

I picked the card up and made up my mind right there that I would definitely be crying on more than just the officer's shoulders. I hoped to be in his bed calling out his name. He didn't make the kind of bread I wanted a nigga to be making, and I wasn't feeling the fact that he was a cop; but there was something there worth exploring. I had every intention on finding out just how far he was willing to go.

Before long, all of the cops came and went. The coroners took Marshall's body away and I answered their questions as best as I could. They asked me all kinds of shit. They asked me if I knew Marshall had a drug problem. They asked me if I knew who was supplying him to get his high.

I told each of them the same story over and over and threw in some fake tears for good measure. I was surprised they let me go. That bitch in blue, Officer

Shiloh, didn't set well with me. I heard her asking her partner, Officer Kern, if he believed me. She told him she felt like I was hiding something.

I sure hoped that bitch minded her own business because I ain't want any problems with the police; especially not her ass. She seemed like she would be a problem I definitely did not want or need.

Let's Try This Shit Again!

I was pleasantly surprised that the cops had let my ass go. I was grateful as hell though. It had been one full week since Marshall tangoed with a tainted dose of his own medicine. I hated a weak man; and he was definitely a weak one and I was glad his bitch ass was gone.

There was only thing wrong...well two. I was broke and after I had ridded myself of Marshall, I didn't know what I was supposed to do next. I was torn between calling Adekite and Officer Kern. I knew what Adekite would do for me. He was strong and made me see I was strong too! He pushed me higher than I had ever been and being that close to my goal of having what I wanted turned me on. He represented the power I wanted. That dude is a Boss and I wanted to rise to the top. He was dangerous and I loved it. Now that the deed was done, I contemplated contacting him. I just didn't know what to say to him.

Then on the other hand, there was Officer Tieriek

Kern who had so unselfishly given me his shoulder to cry on if I needed it. The downfall with him was that he was a fucking cop, and I wasn't quite ready to cozy up around one yet. I did just kill my boyfriend after all.

Rasaun and Nee Nee had been calling and they went straight to voicemail. I ain't have no answers for them about Marshall's death and I wasn't going to talk to them about it either. I spent the week wandering around my empty house. On day number eight, I decided to call Adekite since I had calmed down and it seemed the police weren't going to give me too much static since the autopsy report showed that Marshall had plenty of shit in his system. Apparently, his ass was poppin' Mollies, trying to fight off his sickness. His dumb ass was addicted to anything he could get his greedy hands on. Had he not been dipping in Adekite's stash, none of this shit would have happened.

I found Adekite's number in my cell phone log and called him. Now, what the fuck was I supposed to be say to him? I couldn't blurt out over the phone about what I had done and what had gone down. You never could tell who was listening in.

The phone rang in my ear. Just before I hit the end button, Adekite answered.

"Come to me now, and then we can talk," he said and then the line went dead.

I felt invigorated. He wanted to see me. I got out of the bed and stepped over the exact spot where Marshall's soul departed and entered the throws of Hell. I thought about when I would be joining him in Hell and I shuddered a bit. The cold chill ran up my spine.

Oh, well, fuck it! I might as well do whatever I can to enjoy my life now 'cause God don't like ugly, and I knew damn well He was going to turn me away from the pearly gates.

I shook off the thoughts and decided to live it up while I could, and deal with the consequences later. I showered and dressed. I felt better after bathing. It was like I washed away the bad that was growing inside of me. I found a vintage mint and navy blue dress that I had never popped the tags on. Another gift from the *not so dearly departed* Marshall.

I wiggled my body into the dress and loved the way it hugged my curves. I was definitely cornbread fed. My tits sat up in the dress and the colors and fabric accentuated my creamy complexion and long dark locks. The mint colored, peep-toe pumps made my backside look like it had some weight on it.

Looking in the mirror, I could see the roots of my hair and the brown peeking through. I made a mental note to find someone who could hook my hair up. I damn sure couldn't go back to see Bianca at Hell Razors. My little incident with Erica may not have been so easily forgiven. Knowing Bianca, she didn't care what I had done to Erica; she was most likely pissed about me tearing up her shop. I didn't know how she might react if I waltzed up in there like nothing happened.

I liked everything about the new me and that included my makeover—inside and out. I had to make sure my outside appearance matched what I was feeling on the inside. I felt wild and free of my former self. My old brown locks reminded me of who I used to be, and I didn't want any parts of her. Samantha was gone. I made up my mind I was going to embrace Powder. Embracing the new me was going to be what I was going to live for. I would use Samantha when I saw fit to do so.

I went through my normal routine of being searched. This time it was Ohruh who searched me before leading me to Adekite. Ohruh acted nothing like his brothers. He was the calm to their dark storm. He didn't seem like he would harm a fly. However, this time I was nervous; but for other reasons. This is the first time I have seen Adekite since killing Marshall. There was no telling what he my do to me.

I was led out to the pool area. Adekite was on the deck staring at the ripples in the water. Ohruh announced me and left.

"Come Samantha."

I did as I was asked and I went to Adekite. I took a seat. His gaze never left the pool. "I take it, it is done or you would not have come to me."

"Yes, it is done. I did what you wanted me to do but..." Adekite cut me off before I could tell him about that female cop.

"There are no buts in this line of work. Either you did it, or you didn't," Adekite said, finally looking in my direction. He had a deep scowl on his face that said I had better say I had completed my task.

"Yes! Yes, I did it. Marshall is dead," I said.

"Good," he said, turning his attention back to the pool. "You know what I like about the water? It is calm and if it is undisturbed, it remains calm. However, if there is a storm, the water can be a dangerous force. Samantha, I like calm. I am saying that to say that there shall be no waves nor storms in my organization. I want calm around me. I am letting you in because you have proven yourself worthy. My brother does not want me to allow you inside. I think there is a place for you here. I am sure of it. Just don't make me regret my decision or I will kill you! Do you understand me?"

I nodded my head. I was too afraid to speak.

"Good. You and I will toast to new business, among other things," he said. I could see the crazy behind his eyes, but I could also see the lust in them too.

Something about Adekite was dangerous and it turned me on.

An older woman entered the pool area with two plates of food in her hands. She sat the plates down and left. Another woman appeared with two glasses and a bottle of wine. The food on the plates was not very appealing, but it smelled delicious, so I dug in with Adekite watching me carefully.

"I love a woman who likes to eat. In my country, we like our women thick and healthy. Now that we have gotten all of our issues out of the way, let's get down to business," Adekite said, becoming serious again.

I stopped eating my food and waited for him to tell me what position I would be playing.

"Samantha, for the jobs I need you to do, I need you to get a passport. You will be flying in and out of the country transporting my product for me. This is a risky business, I am sure you know that though. It requires you to stay out of all trouble and keep your shit clean. Do you understand?"

I nodded my head.

"Good! You will be travelling with my brother, Katavious. He is able to move in and out of Nigeria with my product without running the risk of someone finding out what is going on. My contact at the TSA will make sure that you get in and out of the country with no problems and no searches of your belongings."

After hearing what I would be doing, I wasn't as happy as I was before. I hated Katavious and he hated me too. I didn't want to deal with him in any fashion, but if that is what I would have to do to come up, then I was all in.

"Samantha, there are many perks for joining me. I hope you allow me to show you the benefits of this job." Adekite spoke with the same lustful look he had given me before. His eyes dropped to the dangerously low neckline of my dress. He was no doubt checking me out and it made me feel warm and tingly.

I don't know where I got my boldness from, but I eyed Adekite seductively. He was about to find out he wasn't the only lion in this jungle. I stood up and unfastened my dress and let if fall to my feet. I didn't care that we were outside and that his staff or his brothers could possibly see what was about to go down on the deck of the pool. I moved to where he had stopped eating his meal and dropped to my knees. With one swift motion, I unfastened his linen pants and pulled out his monstrous dick. I had never seen anything so black and beautiful before. It was as thick as my wrist and as long as a ruler. This man gave new meaning to the term, *Mandingo*.

With just my touch I felt his manhood swell to massive proportions. I locked eyes with him like a lion does his prey to let him know I was in control of this part. When Adekite's head rolled back from the hand job I was giving him, I knew I had him where I wanted him. I took his tool between my lips and sucked him off like my life depended on it. I didn't think his already huge dick could get any bigger, but the longer I teased and tasted him, the more it swelled. Adekite moaned in delight from the premium head I was laying on him. He couldn't take it anymore, and yanked me to my feet and bent me over the table where our food sat growing cold. Adekite growled and pushed his thickness into me roughly, causing me to wince in pain. I have never been one to back down from a sexual challenge so I gritted my teeth until the pain of being penetrated by his massive dick went from pain to pleasure.

Quickly catching the rhythm, I wound my hips on him. Our bodies collided together making a slapping sound that turned me on even more.

"Oh, shit, yeah!" I moaned, holding myself up on the table top with one hand and rubbing my swollen bud with the other. The sensation of Adekite thrusting himself in and out of me, coupled with being outside where everyone could see us, took me to a whole different place.

I came so hard I felt weak. I almost collapsed on the

table that was holding me up. Adekite quickened his pace, causing me to shudder. The feeling was incredible. He began to growl again and his whole body tensed up. I knew he was close and if I was going to get another nut, I had better get it quick because I didn't know how much longer Adekite was going to last. I bounced back and forth on him, slamming my body into his until I felt that familiar tingle building. I put my foot up in the chair so Adekite could hit my spot just right. I looked over my shoulder and his head was back and his eyes were closed. His mouth was wide open. I focused on the window right behind us only to see Katavious staring at us with a scowl. His jaw was clinched and his eyes bore into me like daggers. Adekite was so wrapped up in fucking me that he didn't see the smile that crossed my lips.

I knew Katavious hated that I was having my way with his brother and that heightened my arousal to new peaks. I closed my eyes and I came so hard I could feel my nectar run down my thigh. Adekite pulled his slick tool out of my juicy box and came all over my bare back and ass.

When I opened my eyes, Katavious was gone. I stood up and looked around to see if anyone else had seen us. Not that I cared. As a matter of fact, if they had seen us it would have been better for me. At least then they would know a new boss bitch had just moved to town.

CHAPTER TEN

The Plan

Shit hadn't gone like I thought it was going to go with Adekite. Sure, he kept his word about giving me a job. I had applied for my passport like he had instructed me to do. There was no question about it; Adekite was demanding that I fly out with Katavious as soon as my passport was in my hands. I had to stall him for a little while until the police cleared me of any wrong doing in Marshall's death before I could freely get my travel documents. That damn female cop, Officer Shiloh, tried to make shit hard for me, but after the autopsy came back with all kinds of drugs in Marshall's system, the police went about their business. They chalked his death up as an overdose and no longer felt the need to question me about it anymore.

I thought by fucking Adekite when he demanded, and doing what I was told, when I was told, that Adekite would see that I was loyal and drop this shit about me making runs in and out of the country with his hating ass brother. That was far from what he wanted.

Adekite put chump change in my pockets and he even paid my bills so I could survive, but he was determined to make sure I was prepared to make my runs out of the country. That was all he wanted to talk about; that, and how much he had riding on me making this happen. He reminded me every chance that he got that I owed him.

I couldn't tell him that I was afraid of being caught smuggling drugs because that would have been a sign of weakness, and I definitely didn't want him to think I was weak. I figured once I showed him I was a rider, and that I could handle being his woman, he would drop this shit. I just had to work a little harder. I had already made up my mind I would make a few runs and then I would get out before I got my ass in some trouble I didn't need. I had gotten away with murder; I may not be so lucky with this shit though. I was nervous about the whole situation.

On top of not being able to get out of this trip to Nigeria, I was lonely. I didn't have anyone to talk to, and Adekite didn't want me to have much of a life. He was paranoid that I would get caught up in some shit and ruin his chances of getting his damn drugs.

After Nee Nee found out about Marshall's death, she started to act strange. My phone calls went unanswered and so did my text messages. Maybe it was better that way because I didn't need anyone around that didn't want to be bothered with me. At times I missed her though, but not enough to kiss her ass and beg her to talk to me. I would have preferred to have my friend, but she seemed to be going through the motions, right along with Rasaun, over Marshall's death.

I was sitting in the bedroom I had once shared with my late boyfriend Marshall. I had decided that if Adekite was going to pay for me to live, then I was going to keep the house and make him pay for it. I don't think he minded though. At times he acted like he needed me and at others he acted like I was a thorn in his side.

After the day he and I fucked by the pool, he was obsessed to a certain degree. He made it very clear that I was to answer my phone whenever he called. There was to be no excuses if I didn't. I had to check in with him whenever I left the house and let him know where I was going. But when I wanted to spend time with him, he had some excuse as to why we couldn't.

My cell phone danced along the nightstand and I knew it was no one but Adekite calling to do his morning check in. I picked up the phone and wished I could hit the lottery like I guessed the timing of his phone calls.

"Good morning, Adekite." I yawned into the phone.

"What took you so long to answer the damn phone? I thought I told your white ass before to answer my call on the first ring! You are gonna make me come over there and teach you a lesson!" he barked into the phone. I was unmoved by his behavior. I had gotten used to it. He was always yelling and fussing about something.

"I was asleep," I responded.

"You need to get your ass here now! What we have been waiting for has arrived. You will be flying out in two days. You need to be here within an hour," he demanded and then the phone went dead.

I rolled my eyes up at the ceiling, but I knew I had better get my ass in gear unless I wanted trouble with Adekite. I had already learned that trouble with him was something I did not want. He had made an example of Marshall and I was not going to fall victim to the same fate. Adekite may have needed me for these trips, but he didn't need me bad enough that he wouldn't hesitate to do something god awful to me if I was disobedient.

I got up, even though I dreaded what I was supposed to do. I showered and quickly dressed, taking note of my brown strands peeking from the roots of my hair. I made a mental note to get that shit handled today. I didn't care who fixed it, but I could not continue walking around with my hair looking a hot mess.

My phone started to dance and sing again across the nightstand again. I snatched it up and answered it blindly. No one called me, so I knew it was Adekite again.

"I am on my way. I had to shower," I said, rushing around looking for the keys to Marshall's truck.

"Ms. Underwood, this is Officer Kern...I mean Tieriek Kern. I didn't mean to bother you. I was just thinking of you. I wanted to make sure you were ok. I can call you back if you are busy," he said.

"Oh, hello Officer Kern. I was just going to meet a friend for lunch. You are no bother." I lied.

"What can I do for you?" I said with a wide smile on my face. I knew he and I had made a connection, but after not hearing from him for a while, I thought nothing more of him. I was so engrossed in the situation I was mixed up in with Adekite, that I didn't give Officer Kern another thought.

"I know it really isn't protocol to do this, but I was thinking of you. I don't know if this is proper or not, but I would like to see you again. You know when you have some free time, of course."

I knew there was more to our meeting than just business the day he had responded to the call for Marshall.

"I have to admit you have run across my mind several times since that day too." I gushed into the phone.

I could practically hear him smiling into the phone as we made a date for later that day. I knew if I could have ditched Adekite I would, but there was no chance in that happening. He was all over me like white on rice.

I finished gathering my stuff and headed out the door to meet Adekite and go over the trip to Nigeria. I made it to Montgomery County with about three minutes to spare before Adekite would start blowing up my phone because I hadn't gotten there in the allotted amount of time. I pulled the truck to the front of the house and hopped out. I rushed up the walkway and rang the bell. I was greeted by Ohruh who offered me a warm smile and stepped aside to let me in. Ohruh no longer searched me when I came to the house, but that didn't stop Katavious from doing so.

Ohruh let me know that Adekite and Katavious were waiting on me in Adekite's office. I thanked him and headed to the office. When I walked in, Adekite immediately looked at his watch to make sure I was on time. I hated that he constantly put me on his schedule and would reprimand me if I was late. Only a nigga that was my man had that privilege and he made it very clear that I was just an employee. That didn't stop me from trying to get into position to be his girl though. I wanted to be in his good graces so I could reap the benefits of being his woman.

Katavious and Adekite were both seated at the marble conference table that took up more than half of the space in the office. I took a seat with Katavious to my right and Adekite to my left.

"I don't want to waste valuable time. I have your travel documents and you two are to fly out together in forty-eight hours. You will pack very light. No more than one suitcase. Katavious will carry the bag with the money that is supposed to be given to our supplier. If anyone asks you, your cover is that you and Katavious have just become engaged and you are flying to Africa to get the blessing of his parents on your union."

I wrinkled my nose up at the thought of getting married to Katavious; even if it was a lie. It was too damn farfetched for me. Anyone who saw Katavious and I interact with one another would know it was a sham! We barely looked at one another, so I didn't know how we were supposed to fly nineteen hours and pretend we were in love when we could barely stand each other.

"You will talk to no one! You will only make small talk when you need to keep outsiders from knowing what you are up to. Katavious will drop you off at the hotel and take it from there. Once he has connected with our contact, you will fly back here two days later. That is when things have the potential to get dangerous." Adekite paused to emphasize the danger of the mission.

I nodded to let him know I fully understood. I hope his asshole brother understood because I didn't want to end up in prison because his brother had a chip on his shoulder.

"Good! My contact at TSA will be the one handling your bags. He will make sure they are not searched. Samantha you are the one who is to retrieve the bags from baggage claim. Not the other way around! This is very important. If Katavious is seen handling those bags it could mean trouble for everyone. It will signal authorities if he does. He will be immediately searched and the bags will be confiscated and we lose everything. Any black man travelling abroad is suspect of smuggling drugs in from Nigeria. Samantha, if he is stopped for any reason at all do not stop. Keep moving. Don't make eye contact with him. Just get the bags and go. If he is searched they will not keep him long. If you do what I tell you, you will be wealthy," Adekite said, staring at me to make sure I understood every word he said.

"I understand." I managed to croak out. I understood what he wanted me to do, but that didn't make me less nervous about it.

He turned and peered at Katavious who did nothing but roll his eyes.

"Is there a problem my brother?" Adekite questioned Katavious, clearly agitated at his behavior.

Katavious pushed away from the table and pointed at me. "I don't know why you trust her. She is a snake. You mark my words, this bitch is going to be our downfall!"

Katavious hissed.

Adekite jumped to his feet and said something in a language I didn't understand. Whatever it was must have been serious because Katavious quieted down. Adekite went to his desk and retrieved an envelope. He re-joined us at the table and placed the envelope in front of me.

"You get half of your money up front and you will get the rest once my package makes it here safely," Adekite said sternly.

I wanted to snatch up the envelope and disappear because these two were too weird me. One of them hated me, and the other one was trying his best to use me without me knowing that was what he was doing. Instead of taking the money, I decided I wanted to get some shit off of my chest. I don't know why I heard Nee Nee's voice from many moons ago playing through my head. I had to stand up for myself or get run over. I was not in the business of being run over anymore, so I had better act like I had some balls and was not going to let Katavious get away with popping off at the mouth about me.

I cleared my throat and spoke up. "Before I accept this job, he needs to respect me. I ain't done shit to him for him to disrespect me like this. He hasn't liked me since day one, and I don't have the slightest idea why. I know one thing though; this shit will never work if he keeps acting like a baby. No one will believe that he and I are in love. We can hardly look at one another without rolling our eyes. How do you expect us to make this happen? I don't see why you didn't send me on this trip with Ohruh. At least I can tolerate him!" I said, cutting my eyes at Katavious who looked like a pot that was about to boil over.

I turned my icy glare towards Adekite. Before I could mumble another word Adekite drew his hand back and smacked me so hard I almost fell from the chair I was seated in. Adekite snatched me by my hair and brought his face so close to mine I could feel his anger oozing from his pores. He forced me to look into his eyes just so I could feel every word he was about to speak.

"Bitch, I call the shots here! You do nothing but what I tell you to do. You will go and get my drugs or I will kill you! You said you wanted to get this money with me; now it is time you prove it!"

Adekite let my hair go and poked me in the chest. I felt the tears welling up in my eyes from him smacking me and snatching me around. I looked around the room only to see Katavious grinning at me. The fact that he was amused by all of this made me hate him even more than I already did.

"I hope I have made myself clear Samantha. There is only one out of this business arrangement and I would hate to show you the exit!" Adekite said regaining my attention.

He shoved the envelope in my chest and pointed for me to leave the office. I got up slowly. My legs felt like jelly while I tried to make it the distance to the door of the office.

Katavious almost fell over. He and Adekite exchanged some words in a foreign language, then they both laughed. Their laughter followed me down the hall and to the front door where I was met by Ohruh.

Ohruh didn't say a word. He looked at me with sorrow etched all over his face. He felt it too, but did not know how to tell me that I had made a grave mistake fucking around with Adekite and Katavious.

CHAPTER ELEVEN

No Use In Crying Over Spilled Milk

I high tailed it out of that house. It took everything in my power to keep me from running from Adekite and Katavious. I had the feeling that even if I ran, they would find me.

Opening the envelope Adekite had given me, I found the passport with my name, ten thousand dollars in cash and my plane tickets to and from Africa. The flight information was booked under Katavious Kyremeh. I stuffed the tickets back in the envelope and tried to push the whole ordeal out of my mind. There was no use in crying over spilled milk. I had already signed up for this bullshit. From the looks of it, there was no way for me to get out of it now. Even the sight of the money didn't excite me. All I could think of was the, *what if's*. What if things didn't go as planned and the authorities searched our stuff? What if something happened in Nigeria and I was arrested there? My mind swirled with different scenarios and how this could all turn out.

I pulled out of the driveway and rounded the corner

when my cell phone began ringing. I maneuvered the steering wheel and looked to see who was calling because I would rather not have to speak to Adekite until the day we were scheduled to leave for Africa. I was elated to see that it wasn't him. In fact, the sight of the name that appeared on the screen made me feel a little better.

"Good afternoon, Officer Kern." I cooed into the phone.

"I didn't expect to hear from you until a little later."

"That is what I am calling about. I may not be able to meet with you until later in the evening. I had a case dropped in my lap and I need to handle some of the details before we can link up. I hope that is aight with you?" Officer Kern said.

"That's fine. I had a few errands to run anyway." I lied. I knew I had ten thousand dollars to play with and if I was going to be forced into making this trip, then I was definitely going to splurge with the money to make myself feel better.

I made plans to meet Tieriek later on and made my way to burn through the money that was lying in the seat next to me. If nothing else would make me feel better, spending some of this money surely would. I spent the rest of the afternoon shopping. I picked up several pieces to wear on the trip that I was not looking forward to. I had even found another salon not too far from my home where I could get my hair colored.

I sat in the unfamiliar shop while the stylist, Keisha, colored the roots of my hair. No matter what shop you went to, the atmosphere was the same. There were cackling females gossiping about the next female. People were in and out of the shop trying to sell their items and the women were giving up their last few coins to buy the knock off items the street vendors were selling. Something about being in the salon was refreshing. It took my mind off of some of my woes.

The women in the shop continued to talk trash about one another and I only half assed paid attention until someone mentioned Marshall's name. I sat up straight in the chair and tried my best not to stare at the older skinny black woman who was talking about her son Marshall. The woman put me in the mind of Momma Dee from Love and Hip Hop. She was tired looking and the weave she was getting sewn into her hair was tasteless. She looked eerily familiar, but since I had never seen any of Marshall's family I couldn't be sure if this woman was his mother or not. Instead, I sat there with my head in a magazine, trying to look like I wasn't listening to their conversation. The woman was telling the story of how her son was found dead, in what used to be his home by the authorities, from a supposed overdose.

"The police said he died from a heroin overdose, but it ain't nothing you can tell me that it wasn't some bitch he was messing around with that killed him. I tell you my son was happy with his life. He would not have turned to drugs. That wasn't his style. He was in the streets, but he was no junkie! I told Marshall that these scandalous women he would mess around with from time to time were going to be the death of him. He would stir up so much shit with them gals that there was no telling what kind of mess he had them believing. He had homes all over the place and was keeping different women in all of them. Some of them knew about the other females and some of them didn't. When I tell you chile it is a mess, it is a mess. The medical examiner just released his body to me. That is when they told me it was a definite case of overdose. I have to prepare for his funeral and figure out all of his assets so I can be done with it all. That boy had houses and cars all over the Tri-state area. It is gonna take me months to get all of this stuff in order," the woman said.

The more I tried to act as though I wasn't listening, the harder it was for me to contain myself. I wanted to ask the woman who her son was, although I already knew the answer. I wanted confirmation, but I didn't dare ask her a thing.

"From what I hear, he was dealing with some trailer park trash. At least that is what the police officer told me. She said that when they found him there was some white woman in his home. I find that hard to believe because Marshall was a lot of things, but a sellout he was not! He would never date outside of our race. If anything, that bitch he was in there with probably had him trying all kinds of shit. You know how *they* do."

Then the old bitch had the nerve to look at me. "No offense honey. There is nothing wrong with dating outside of your race. It's just my son wasn't the type to do it," the old bag had the nerve to say.

I wanted to get in her face and tell her it was me that

was living with her trifling, piece of shit son! I wanted to scream from the top of my lungs that I had killed his sorry ass. I could tell she was a racist bitch trying to act like she wasn't because I was around. I bit down on the inside of my cheek to keep from leaping from my chair and smacking the shit out of her for being an idiot. I knew beating her down would have been the wrong thing to do, although it would have made me feel better to smack her one good time. I knew if I had gotten into yet another fight, I was going to be in more trouble than just the cops bringing me in on some assault charges. I would have to deal with Adekite for getting mixed up in some drama when I was supposed to be avoiding it.

The woman who I assumed was Marshall's mother rambled on and on about her late son and his untimely death. The women in the shop listened as the woman told all of her son's business. Some of them offered her advice on what she should do with all of his things. I listened as they told her to gather up all of Marshall's things and sell them. I was growing more furious by the moment. I could not believe that Marshall had a bitch for a mother and he had other homes all over the place. Hearing that Marshall had other women on the side was no surprise to me because that was the way he operated. He wasn't a one-woman type of man. He had a different bitch for every day of the week. I didn't give a damn about the women. I was pissed that while he was busy getting high and I was stuck selling everything in our home to keep a roof over our heads, that nigga never cared. He had women and homes scattered all around.

If that bastard wasn't dead, I would have killed his sorry ass again.

I was so angry I dug my fingernails into the armrest on the leather chair I was sitting in. I made a vow that I would see Marshall's mother another time and when I did, I would make sure to let her know that her son had been eating my pussy and paying my bills up until the time of his death! Fuck her and him too!

I was more than appreciative that the conversation had switched up to other talk and Marshall's mother had found some other gossip to involve herself in. I wanted to get out of there. I knew Marshall's funeral would be coming up real soon and I didn't know if his nosey mother was going to come snooping around my spot. The last thing I needed was her rolling through with movers talking about I had to go. Luckily for me, she and I had finished our hair up at the same time. I let her walk out before me and I peeped her tag number before she pulled off. I almost broke my heel trying to get to the truck. I needed to write the tag number down before I forgot it.

I unlocked the car and started the engine before I got inside. I hopped in and wrote the number on a bill that needed to be paid and peeled off from the curb. I was able to catch up to her late model Jaguar before she got lost in the traffic. Following three car lengths behind her, I tried to keep up. I wanted to find out where that bitch lived. She had done too much talking and I didn't like what she had to say. I was on a mission when she made it through a light and I was stuck behind some asshole who didn't believe in running yellow lights. I blew the horn at him and flipped his ass the finger for not running the light.

"Fuck!" I yelled. Marshall's mother had disappeared in the traffic. I tried to look at the bright side of things... at least I knew she may be coming to uproot me from my house. I also got her tag number. I might be able to make some shit happen with that.

I made an illegal U-turn in the street and headed in the direction of my house. I still had a date with fine ass Tieriek. He might even be able to get me some information on Marshall's mother's tag. If all else failed, I still had money coming to me once I landed safely back in the U.S. with Adekite's stuff. I could move if I had too. I wasn't trying to move, but it might be in my best interest to have a plan B just in case. I toyed with the idea of moving during the drive back to my house. I didn't have much time before I was supposed to meet Tieriek. I took my bags in the house and popped the tags off the new *DKNY* lamb leather dress I had purchased for an easy thousand dollars. I couldn't help but to get the wedge shoes that matched the dress for another five hundred. I had spent upwards of four grand since Adekite had put the money in my hands earlier in the day. I almost regretted spending that much money after finding out Marshall's mother might be serving me my eviction papers.

Well, even if I felt like crap on the inside, I would look like a million bucks on the outside.

I ran myself a bath and tried to relax my mind. This

had been one stressful ass day. One thing about me though, was that I was like a cat with nine lives. No matter how fucked up my shit might be, I always landed on my feet and hit the pavement running. I intended to do that at all costs. There was no doubt in my mind that I wouldn't either.

I finished my bath and sprayed my favorite *Dolce & Gabbana* perfume before I did my makeup and slid into my dress. I was working the hell out of this dress. I hoped it worked for me in more ways than one. It was twenty minutes before I was supposed to meet Tieriek. We were going to have dinner at Mc Cormick and Schmick's on the waterfront. The sun was setting, but it was a gorgeous Spring night. I was grateful to be spending the evening out. It might take my mind off of my upcoming travel and Marshall's mother.

I made it to the restaurant and didn't feel like finding parking, so I paid the valet to park the truck. When I stepped inside, I spotted Tieriek immediately. He stood and waved me over to where he had been seated. When I reached the table, I noticed he had a bottle of Rosé already waiting.

"Good evening. I'm sorry for being late. I guess I let time get away from me," I said, receiving his embrace. He smelled delicious and he looked good enough to eat. I took note that he cleaned up well out of his uniform. He looked laid back and relaxed and that caused me to relax a bit too.

"I started to think you were going to stand me up. I hope you like Rosé. I took the liberty of ordering it for you. I hope you don't mind."

I took my seat and he poured me a glass. Soon afterwards, the waitress came over and took our order. We spent the whole evening getting to know one another. I had to admit, I was intrigued by him. He was smart and had the potential to do so much more than be a damn cop. I was trying desperately to get pass his occupation and how we'd met. No matter how hard I tried, the fact still remained the same; we played on opposite sides of the field.

We had made it through the entire dinner without mentioning Marshall and his death. We took a stroll out on the boardwalk and enjoyed one another's company until Tieriek asked me about Marshall.

"Samantha, how long was your ex using drugs?"

I cringed when he asked me that question. I didn't want to talk about Marshall. Thoughts of him drudged up other thoughts about Adekite, my very recent encounter with Marshall's mother, and all of the other things I was trying to avoid.

I stopped walking alongside him. I attempted to look sad and replied, "I didn't know he was using drugs until the very end. I guess I was the last to know. Had I known sooner, maybe I could have helped him." I lied.

Tieriek took my hands in his. "Some people just don't want to be helped. I never get used to seeing someone strung out on drugs. It makes me wonder why anyone would try and chase that kind of high. Something in their life has got to be really fucked up to make a person decide to say fuck it and try to solve their problems with drugs. I think that is why I became a cop. I did it to try and help the weak."

I started to walk again. "I saw too much of that shit when I was growing up to make me steer clear of all of it. I saw what it did to my parents and I didn't want any parts of it. That's why when I found out that Marshall had an addiction I was so upset. He told me that he could control it and that he wasn't doing it all the time. I guess I should have known better than that," I said, laying it on really thick.

My little act must have been working because Tieriek looked deep into my eyes and kissed me. It was so innocent and sweet that I forgot that we were out in the open and everyone could see us. I surrendered into his hungry kiss and got lost in the hunger in his lips. When we finally pulled apart from one another, we stared at each other. There was an awkward silence. I couldn't help but to giggle nervously.

"Damn, are my skills that bad that you had to laugh at a brother?" he asked laughing at his own joke.

I shook my head. "Nawh, I just never thought I would date a cop. Especially a cop that I met under the circumstances I met you under."

"Does my being a police officer bother you?" he asked me seriously.

"No, but I haven't been totally honest with you, Tieriek. I like you, and I don't want you to judge me for mistakes I may have made in the past because they are just that...my past and ain't nobody perfect." I was setting shit up for the kill.

Tieriek looked at me confused and I swear I saw a glimmer of fear at what he thought he was about to learn about me.

"Look, I didn't know that Marshall was using drugs. I did know that he was selling them though. I knew he had some older woman that would stop pass the house and make his runs for him. I knew what he was doing was wrong, but I didn't have a choice but to go along with whatever Marshall said and did. I was stuck in between a rock and a hard place. It was either go along with it or be homeless. I decided that I would rather have a roof over my head than live in the streets," I said, hoping he was buying all of the bullshit I was feeding him. I studied his face and it looked like he believed me.

"Let me ask you something Samantha, and you don't have to tell me if you don't want to tell me, but do you know who the woman was that your boyfriend was doing business with? Did you know the woman who was helping him and do you think she would have any reason to slip him a hot dose?" Tieriek asked taking the bait. I had him right where I wanted him.

"All I have is her tag number. I know the woman drives a late model Jaguar and she looked to be in her forties or fifties. I can't really tell you much more than that. Marshall was real quiet about his business dealings." I lied.

The truth was I didn't know shit about the woman besides she was definitely Marshall's mother. I didn't even know her first name. It figures though, because Marshall was doing way too much in the streets and the less we both knew...the better off I guess he thought we would be. Little did he know that it was going to work in my favor that he kept so many women and so many secrets. I tried to contain myself from laughing. I was thinking about setting up Marshall's mother and it was hilarious to me. I bet she wouldn't be so quick next time to run her mouth and tell all of her business!

"Hello...Samantha, what are you smiling for?" Tieriek watched me curiously while I tried to wipe the grin off of my face.

"Oh, nothing...just a memory of Marshall that ran across my mind. What were you saying?" I tried to get him back on the subject of running this bitches tags and taking her in for questioning. I needed him to detain her ass until I could find another spot to live. I didn't need her running her mouth about me. The heat had finally died down from Marshall's death. I didn't need her to get Officer Shiloh riled up about me again.

"Oh, I hope me asking you out wasn't too soon for you. I know you losing your boyfriend the way you did was tragic," Tieriek said sincerely.

I felt all warm inside. He was so caring it was kind of scary. I had gotten used to men like Marshall who thought everything was about him. All Marshall wanted from me was to do what he said and leave him alone. He wanted a trophy bitch. I fell in love with being obedient for the monetary means. I forgot about me in the process of trying to be kept.

"Hey, do you know how to skate?" Tieriek asked.

"Yeah...why?"

"I was thinking about going skating. You better not laugh either, but I love to skate. Maybe on our next date we can go skating," Tieriek said, already planning to see me again.

I blushed. I know my cheeks were red as a beet. I hated that shit too. Niggas could always tell when they made me feel a certain kind of way. My feelings were literally written all over my face.

"Sure, I would love to go skating with you."

"Good. I have to work tomorrow. How about the day after tomorrow we find a rink and I watch you bust your ass?" Tieriek laughed.

The smile faded from my face. I wasn't going to be in town. Hell, I wasn't going to be in the country in two days. I had to make up some shit to tell him to keep him from knowing anything about what I would be doing and where I would be.

"I won't be available. Can we do it next week? I got a few things I have to take care of. I have to check on my mother." The lies were flowing so easily from my lips. Had I not known they were lies, I would have believed them too.

Tieriek's face showed his disappointment. I wish I could have gone out with him sooner, but I had other things I was obligated to do. I needed the money so I knew I had to follow through with Adekite's plans for me. Even if I didn't need the money, Adekite wasn't going to let me back out anyway.

My cell phone started to ring in my bag. I knew I had better see who it was because if it was Adekite and

I didn't answer, he would start acting a fool. He would keep calling until I answered. I fished my phone from my bag and saw it was Nee Nee. I don't know why I felt relieved to see her name, but I was. I answered before she was sent to voicemail.

"Hey, stranger. I haven't heard from you in about a month," I said before she could even say hello.

"Hey, Powder. I have been with Rasaun. You know he is taking Marshall's death kind of hard. He's been all fucked up."

I took a few steps away from Tieriek so he couldn't hear what I was saying.

"Damn. I'm sorry to hear that. Hey, listen, what are you doing tomorrow? I miss ya' girl."

Nee Nee hesitated. "I don't know. Rasaun seems like he is feeling better, so I might be able to creep away. Plus, I need to talk to you. I have something I need to ask you. Meet me tomorrow at the Pavilion. Let's make it about one o'clock okay?"

I told Nee Nee I would see her the following day. I wanted to know what she had to ask me. I hoped it was nothing about Marshall.

I walked back over to Tieriek.

"I'm sorry about that. I was waiting on that call." I smiled.

He took my hand in his again and we continued to stroll along.

"You seem like you're a very busy lady. I hope you promise to make time for me in your life. I know I can't replace your folks, but I can try to mend your broken heart," Tieriek said while we strolled hand in hand.

I couldn't respond before he scooped me into his arms and kissed me long and deep. I relaxed. The stress of Marshall, his mother and Katavious and Adekite all left my body. When we finally pulled apart from one another, I was breathless. I don't know why I felt like I was being watched. I looked around nervously.

"I'm sorry Samantha. I hope I wasn't out of line. I couldn't help it. I wanted to do that since the day I met you."

All of a sudden I felt out of place. I know Tieriek was getting tired of my erratic behavior, but if he really knew all I had going on he would surely understand. I figured I would rather end the date and end it on a good note than continue to act like a paranoid freak.

Tieriek was such a gentleman, he said he understood. We went our separate ways and when I got into the truck I had the same feeling again. I felt like someone was watching me. I looked all around hoping I could find the presence that had me freaking out. I was unsuccessful in my attempt. There was no one around that I could identify. I shrugged it off and pulled away from the valet station, anticipating my next chance to see Tieriek.

I didn't know it then, but I had good reason to feel like someone was watching me. Little did I know someone was lurking in the shadows checking for me.

Friend Or Foe

I woke up several times in the middle of the night. Every time I closed my eyes I saw Marshall's face. He threatened to tell Tieriek that I was the one who had killed him and not the drugs. I would wake up screaming and begging for Marshall not to tell Tieriek. The dream was so vivid that I would wake up and the pillow would be soaked from my tears.

This time when I woke up I decided to stay up. There was no need in going back to bed and subjecting myself to the torture all over again. Besides, I didn't have much time before I was supposed to meet up with Nee Nee. I put on my silk robe and headed to the kitchen and made a pot of coffee. I sat at the table sipping my black coffee and pulling on a *Newport* while thinking of all the shit I had to do. I still hadn't packed one stitch of clothing and I was due to leave the next morning. I went through the classified section of the Washington Post hoping to find some place to live that seemed appealing and most of all...affordable.

After my coffee and marking a few places I planned to check out when I got back, I got my ass in gear and starting sifting through my closet. I made a mental note to remove all of Marshall's shit as soon as I got back. I was sick of being reminded of him. It bugged me to no end that even though he was dead, he still called the shots; he still haunted my dreams and the nigga was taking up space in the closet. As far as I was concerned, he was a thorn in my side even in death.

I pulled out a few things I would take with me to Africa. I didn't know what I was going to need. This wasn't a vacation, this was business. All I knew was that I needed to pack light. I didn't think I was going to be going anywhere special. I had no intentions on being around Katavious while we were away, so I didn't see any need to take too much. I made up my mind that I was going to stay away from him until we had to deal with one another. I'm sure he wouldn't have any objections about it either. I figured I would talk to Adekite about what he thought I would need for the trip. I knew he would be contacting me before the day was out. It would be a miracle if he didn't.

I finished rummaging through my clothing and found a pair of Seven7 jeans and a simple blouse to wear out to meet Nee Nee. I was excited to see my friend, but I couldn't help but wonder what she needed to talk to me about. We hadn't spoken since I called to tell her that Marshall was dead. That was going on a solid month.

Twenty minutes later, I was sitting in the Pavilion waiting on Nee Nee to arrive. When she finally did she didn't look like herself. She looked around cautiously before taking a seat across from me. She didn't look like the vibrant Nee Nee I had seen last. She looked like she had lost weight and her appearance was lacking the flair she normally possessed. She was rocking a pair of sweatpants and an oversized t-shirt that looked as if it had swallowed her whole.

Nee Nee shuffled over to the table and eyed me suspiciously. The hair on the back of my neck stood at attention. Something about the way she looked at me troubled me.

"Hi, Samantha," Nee Nee said dryly, which put me further on edge. Nee Nee never called me Samantha. Since the day we met, she had called me Powder.

"Wow, when did we start being so formal?" I quizzed her. Her discomfort was making me uncomfortable too. I wanted her to tell me what was going on. I hated playing cat and mouse games. My time was valuable and I couldn't afford to have her or anyone else waste it.

"Look, Powder, I need to know what the hell happened with Marshall. I promised Rasaun that I would find out what I could."

I watched her closely because I was looking to see if she showed any signs of knowing what really went down with Marshall the day of his death.

"Nothing happened. He was a junkie posing to be a hustler. He got caught slipping because he started using his own product and I guess he OD'd. Case closed," I said nonchalantly, hunching my shoulders.

"Samantha, I don't know what happened in that

house with you and Marshall, but Rasaun and his mother want answers. You are gonna have to tell them something! So, no, the case ain't closed!"

I could feel my blood starting to boil. Who the fuck did Nee Nee think she was trying to tell me what to do? Besides, I didn't have to answer to anyone about anything. I started to tell Nee Nee about Marshall's mother and me seeing her in the salon. I decided against it since Nee Nee clearly had beef and I couldn't tell whose side she was on.

"I don't know what the hell they think I'm gonna be able to tell them besides the same thing I just told you."

Nee Nee raised her perfectly arched eyebrows and tapped her manicured figures across the table like she didn't believe anything I had told her. I could see she was growing impatient with me and I really didn't care. I didn't know what she expected me to tell her, but I knew what I wasn't going to say.

"Samantha, how could you live with a man for months on end and not know he was using? I just don't believe you ain't know shit about him having a habit. You knew about every female he fucked and you kept tabs on his money, but you didn't know he was getting high? That shit makes no sense to me. I hope you plan on making me understand this shit."

I wasn't feeling her interrogation. I decided to tell her enough to get her off my back. "Shaunie, I'm gonna keep it real with you. I noticed Marshall was dipping in the cookie jar a few months ago. The first time I caught him messing around with the shit was the day I had the altercation in the salon. I asked him about it and he went off on me. He damn near choked me to death because I had come at him wrong. He told me to mind my business and that he only got high to take the edge off. I thought he had it all under control. I guess he didn't. From then on, I would notice he was getting high all the time. He couldn't function. All he did was shovel that shit up his nose. I threatened to tell Rasaun and Marshall told me that if I told anyone what was going on in our home he would kill me." I sniffled. I started to tear up to give the illusion that I gave a damn about Marshall and his drug habit.

"What was he using Samantha? Was he using the shit he was selling or was he using something else?" She continued to quiz me.

That was my breaking point. I don't know who the fuck she thought she was asking me all of these questions. I didn't even get the third degree like this when the police asked me questions about Marshall's death. Nee Nee had some damn nerve.

"I don't know what's going on here *Shaunie*, but I don't think I like it. I wasn't the one who gave him the shit. You know how I feel about drugs of any kind! You, of all people, know what I went through with my parents. I didn't hold a gun to his fucking head and make him use the shit. Maybe if you and Rasaun were better friends you would have known the nigga had a problem from the door instead being Johnny Come Lately and trying to tell me what I could have done better. You need to be pointing the finger at yourself. His blood is on my hands just like it's on yours if we are basing his death on who should have helped save him. You were supposed to be his friends too!" I fumed.

I snatched up my bag off of the table and prepared to make my exit. I didn't like where this conversation was going. It had me beyond frustrated.

"Powder, you can save all of the dramatics. I had to ask for myself what happened to him. I told you I ain't the only one who believes there is more to this story... but they ain't ya friend. They aren't gonna ask you shit! They are gonna shoot first and ask questions later. A lot of money got fucked up in the streets because of Marshall's death. Not to mention he did have family and friends who cared about him," Nee Nee said, raising her voice.

My heart started to thump hard and fast. I was furious now. "Like I said, Marshall was fucked up and it ain't have nothing to do with me. You can tell whoever thinks otherwise I said so! The police cleared me of any wrong doings because I didn't do anything wrong!" I stood up and Nee Neee must have thought I was challenging her because she jumped to her feet and got in a defensive stance. I shook my head and pulled my shades over my eyes.

"This was a complete waste of my time. I thought you were my friend! Instead, after a month and some change you come here with this bullshit. You, Rasaun and whoever else thinks I had something to do with that junkie ass nigga dying can kiss my lily white ass. All I'm gonna tell you is the same thing I told everyone else...

prove it!" I screamed at the top of my lungs. Nee Nee had taken me there!

Nee Nee stood there with a ferocious anger beginning to build. It could have been because of the way I had spoken to her, or because she really couldn't do anything about it in such a public place without making more of scene. She stood there like the well-trained puppy she was. Shaunie was a lot of things, but I would have never thought she would have brought me here to play detective and try and question me. I stormed away from her and didn't feel an ounce of regret for how I spoke to her. I could feel the eyes of every person in the Pavilion on me. I know Shaunie and I had put on a huge show for all of the common folks who gathered at the Pavilion to enjoy the peace and tranquility it normally offered. That was all shattered now.

I don't know why I expected her to be right behind me, but she wasn't. I held my head high as I strutted out. I didn't care what any of those people thought of what had just transpired. They should have been minding their own damn business anyway. I tossed my golden-colored locks and put a twist in my hips since I had an audience. I fast walked to the truck and hopped inside. I made an executive decision right there. I was definitely moving up out of Marshall's shit. I had made more enemies than enough just by ridding myself of Marshall. I had gotten rid of one problem and gained three more. I was a sitting duck. There was no telling who was going to come looking for me because of him. His mother was already making plans on selling all of his stuff. Rasaun was mourning his dead friend and seeking revenge and Nee Nee had a chip on her shoulder. I guess it was a good thing I was going to be gone for a few days so I could clear my head. I had a long flight to and from Nigeria to figure out what I was going to do next.

I pulled away from the Pavilion with one thing on my mind. I needed to make this money so I could get the hell out of DC. Nee Nee had made it clear that no one believed Marshall's death was an accidental overdose. One thing for sure, I wasn't going to sit around and wait for them to come looking for me!

A Decision To Make

I went home and immediately packed everything I had intended to take with me to Africa. I smoked a blunt to calm my nerves and clear my head because if I didn't, I may have gone insane. The stunt Nee Nee pulled earlier had me on edge, but I still had to do what I had to do. Adekite was far more of a threat than Nee Nee and Rasaun.

I had packed up almost everything I thought I would need and I sat down on the couch with a drink and the rest of my blunt. I tried my hardest to relax, but the thought of Marshall's mother bursting through the front door and ordering me to get out kept surfacing in my thoughts. I didn't feel safe in my home anymore. I decided that I was not going to stay there another night. I got my suitcases that I intended to take with me on my trip and headed out the front door. I would deal with my living situation when I landed back on U.S. soil safely. Who even knew if things would go as smoothly as Adekite and Katavious had planned. What if we got caught? I wouldn't have to worry about a place to live because the State would furnish a place for me to live for a minimum of five years in a prison if I got caught.

I drove to a hotel that was close to the airport that Katavious and I were supposed to fly out from. I hated driving to Baltimore. It was too far and the police looked at everyone like they were a suspect. I figured I might as well spend the night closer to the airport since my flight was in the morning and I didn't want to be in the house anyway.

Surprisingly, the further I got away from the city, the better off I started to feel. By the time I pulled into the Hilton I had almost forgotten about everything that was troubling me back in DC. The sun had finally set and the planes were flying overhead. I couldn't help but think that tomorrow I would be on one of those planes. I had never flown before. Hell, I had barley gotten out of the city. If it weren't for relatives from time to time taking pity on me when I was younger, I probably would have never gotten out of the city at all.

I checked into my room and dropped off my bags and decided to try G and M Restaurant and Lounge. I had heard Nee Nee talk about how amazing their seafood was and wanted to see for myself. I didn't bother to change my clothes. I hoped that my jeans, blouse and heels were appropriate because I had no idea if the place had a dress code or what. I pulled up in front of the place and it didn't look like much on the outside, but I was pleasantly surprised when I got inside and was finally seated. The décor was beautiful and the food was absolutely delicious. I took the liberty of ordering several drinks to take the edge off.

By the time I made it back to my hotel I was tipsy as hell with not a care in the world about the shit going on in my life. I stripped down naked and passed out in the room somewhere around 11:00 p.m., only to be awakened by the sounds of my phone ringing around 2:00 a.m. I was super pissed because I hadn't slept that good since before I had killed Marshall. I took the phone and answered without looking at the screen.

There were several clicks on the line.

"Hello? Hello," I said, growing furious that someone had broken my rest.

No one said anything. I was about to hang up when I heard the weird clicking again. I shrugged it off as a wrong number because a number I didn't know appeared on the screen.

"I ain't got time for this shit!" I said groggily and hung up.

I had turned over and was settling back down to drift off back into my drunken slumber when the phone rang again. This time I looked at the screen and saw the same number from before and answered it. This time I was going to give this mother fucka' a piece of my mind.

"Hello! If you want to play games on my phone you could at least wait until a bitch is wide awake. You ain't got shit better to do than play on my phone. I know you are lonely and need some attention. You need someone's voice to choke your chicken to?" I laughed.

There was laughter from the other end of the line. I

couldn't tell if it was a man or a woman because it was muffled. Then I heard the most chilling words I think I had ever heard in my young life.

"Bitch, you're dead!" the voice said and then the line went dead. The hair on the back of my neck stood up like it always did when I was uncomfortable. I sat staring into space wondering who would call me and make that kind of a threat. I knew Nee Nee and Rasaun were upset about Marshall, but I couldn't see him being that mad. Nee Nee and I were mad at one another but I didn't think she would stoop that low. She wasn't the petty type to play on the phone. I was still buzzing from the drinks so I couldn't catch the voice; I could only make out that it was a woman...who I didn't know.

While sitting there trying to figure out who would make such a threat, my phone rang again.

"Who the fuck is this and why the fuck do you keep calling me?" I shouted into the phone.

"Who do you think you are talking to Samantha? I don't know what is going on with you, but you had better get your shit together. You have important business to handle in the morning and I need you focused!" Adekite growled into the phone.

"Oh, it's you. I'm...I'm sorry. I thought you were someone else," I said. I refrained from telling him the whole truth because I knew he wouldn't approve or he wouldn't care. All he was focused on was getting his drugs so he could make his money. That was all he cared about.

"Where the fuck are you? Ohruh went past your house and said you weren't there. I hope you aren't trying to pull any of your slick shit because if you are...I will hunt you down and I will do things to you far worse than your worst nightmare, bitch!"

If I wasn't awake before from the first calls, I was definitely awake now. I was trembling at the sound of his voice. From the way he threw his threats, I knew his words were promises.

"I'm going to ask you once again, where are you?" He sounded off into the phone.

I sat up and fought back the bile that was threatening to leave the confines of my stomach and land all over the Hilton's sheets from the alcohol I had earlier in the evening.

"I'm at the Hilton by Baltimore Washington International Airport. I wanted to be closer to the airport." I stammered, trying to explain myself before Adekite grew angrier.

"Good. Good girl. Glad you were thinking ahead. Next time you better let me know when you think you are going to be making anymore sudden moves," he chuckled deviously into the phone.

I shivered from hearing him switch up like Dr. Jekyll and Mr. Hyde.

"Samantha, don't make me kill you. If you do what I say, you will make a lot of money. If you fuck up, I will kill you! Have a good night."

Click.

The line went dead. The food and drinks from earlier came up splattering all over the comforter and the pillow. I jumped up and booked to the bathroom to

BlaQue

finish tossing my dinner and cocktails up in the toilet. Once I finished, I stepped out of my soiled clothes and started the shower. Walking naked into the sleeping area, I took a seat on the recliner and called the front desk.

"Can you send someone to change my linen please? I had an accident. As a matter of fact can you put in a wakeup call for 7:00 a.m. please? I also need laundry service."

I hung up and showered until the shower ran cold. By the time I got out, the maid had come and gone. She had changed the sheets and taken the soiled clothes I requested to be cleaned. I lay across the bed and drifted into an uneasy sleep. This time when I closed my eyes it wasn't peaceful as it had been before. Adekite and Marshall flooded my dream, turning it into a nightmare. They were both standing over me and I couldn't move. I didn't know how they had gotten into my room. My hands and legs were bound. I tried frantically to get free, but wasn't doing anything but wearing myself out. It was of no use. I wasn't going anywhere. Marshall looked like he did before he started using drugs. He was clean and sober. He looked so handsome. The tears slipped from my eyes. I begged Marshall to have mercy on me, but he wouldn't say a word. He acted like he couldn't hear me. Adekite pulled a pistol out of his waistband and handed it to Marshall. He guided Marshall's hand and placed the barrel of the gun to my temple forcefully, causing me to wince from the pressure. Adekite walked away and took a seat and kicked his feet up on the hotel desk.

"Do this bitch!" Adekite ordered. Marshall looked into my eyes and I could see a piece of him that actually cared for me.

"Marshall, I'm so sorry baby. I never meant to hurt you!" I cried.

He smiled his crooked smile that had me hooked from the first time I met him. I thought maybe, just maybe, he would feel something for me and not do as he was being ordered to do. Instead, he pulled the hammer back and squeezed the trigger.

I woke up in a sweat and screaming. The sheets were stuck to my wet body. The hotel phone rang and I screamed again, startled by the sound. My heart thumped in my chest. I snatched up the phone.

"Yeah?" I said breathlessly into the desk phone. I almost dropped it, my body shook so violently.

"Ms. Underwood, this is your wakeup call. Also, your laundry is ready. Would you like for us to bring it to you, or would you like to pick it up when you check out?" the clerk asked.

"You can have someone bring it up. I would appreciate that," I said nervously.

The clerk hesitated and asked me was everything okay. I quickly told her I was fine and hung up.

I've got to calm the fuck down! I thought. I gathered my belongings and pulled on my clothes.

I even took the time to make that nasty hotel coffee that they leave in each room. I needed something that would settle me down. My stomach was in knots. After the third sip of the coffee that didn't have enough sugar or cream, I poured it down the sink. The concierge knocked on the door with my clean clothes and took my suitcase. I stuffed my clean clothes in my carry-on and followed the old man to the front desk. I secretly hoped that I would never be his age and working at a hotel like he was. There couldn't be any money in that.

He sat my bags down next to me and I pressed a twenty dollar bill in his palm for carrying my suitcase. I don't know why I gave him such a large tip. I guess I was trying to make my good deeds outweigh the bad ones. I checked out, got in the truck and booked it the short ride to the airport. It was *do or die* and I had no choice but to go through with this shit or have Adekite kill me for not doing it.

Lagos, Nigeria

I made it to BWI and went through airport security without any problems. Not that I thought I would have any issues leaving the country. It was my returning to the United States that had me nervous and ready to tuck my tail between my legs and run. I had to *dead* those thoughts because no matter where I tried to run, Adekite would find me. No sooner than I had thought about Adekite, Katavious wandered to where I was sitting waiting to board our flight. Seeing Katavious made me feel a little bit better. I still hated him, but if I was going down for this shit there was no doubt in my mind that he would be coming with me. I wasn't going to take these charges on my own.

Katavious nodded in my direction and took a seat next to me. He wore a huge grin across his face that instantly had me on edge. He had never smiled at me before and it gave me the creeps. I swallow the lump that was forming in my throat and tried to play it cool. He and I had to spend the next seventy-two hours with one another, and that didn't include the flight to and from Nigeria. I figured I might as well make the best of it because he was stuck with me like I was stuck with him. Neither one of us was happy about it, but it had to be done. The only difference between us was that Katavious was a willing participant and my hand was being forced.

"Glad to see you made it," Katavious finally said through his fake smile.

"I didn't have much of a choice now did I?" I shot back.

Katavious chuckled. "You're right about that. You had absolutely no choice in the matter."

Katavious leaned over and kissed me on the cheek and threw his strong arms around me. I squirmed from the gestures. I almost got up and changed seats and I thought about the mission at hand. We were supposed to be a young couple in love. I sucked my teeth and bit down hard on my cheek trying to deal with Katavious. He made my skin crawl.

We finally boarded our flight and we were flying First Class. I was thankful for the room, but I would have gladly flown coach if it meant I could get the hell away from this sly ass nigga I was being forced to smuggle drugs with. I took out my Kindle and scanned it to find something that would keep me distracted during the flight. I found a book called Hackin' and Stackin', by some guy named, George Sherman Hudson, who I had heard about. I hope it took the entire flight for me to read it because I didn't want to have to interact with

Katavious.

There was no need to worry because by the time we were in the air and the flight attendant, who introduced herself as Margo, came rolling through our section with cocktails, I had ordered three of them. We had only been in the air for all of thirty minutes.

Margo explained that there was an in-flight movie and that if I needed anything else I should let her know. No sooner than she had set the third drink in front of me, I knew I was going to need something stronger than these drinks to keep me calm. I explained to Margo that it was my first time flying and that I was nervous. She reached inside her apron pocket and pulled out a green pill and slipped it to me so no one could see what she was giving me.

"This will take care of your discomfort." Margo winked at me. She didn't move, so I reached in my purse and handed her a crisp twenty and she rolled her cart along the aisle as if nothing had transpired between the two of us. I looked around to make sure no one had seen what we did and no one seemed to care or notice. Even Katavious was clueless to the exchange. I wasn't big on taking any type of drug—over the counter or from the streets—so I was apprehensive on taking the little green pill. I tucked the pill into my purse and hoped I didn't need it. I tried to focus on the movie, but when the plane hit some turbulence I got up and rushed to the little bathroom. I popped the pill in my mouth and washed it down with some water from the sink.

I sure hope that in-flight drug pusher hadn't slipped me

anything crazy. I thought. I guess it was too late to worry about it now because I was thousands of miles in the air.

I straightened out my clothes and headed back to my seat. The last thing I remember was the opening credits of the movie Face-Off with John Travolta and Nicolas Cage. I fell fast asleep and didn't wake up until Katavious shook me eighteen hours later when our plane had taxied the runway in Lagos, Nigeria.

As I exited the plane, Margo was assisting an elderly passenger off the plane. I fell behind Katavious and waited for Margo to catch up. There was no way I was going to make it through the fight back without the little green pill Margo had given me. Katavious had gone ahead towards baggage claim. Margo gave me a knowing nod and walked over to where I stood waiting for her.

"How was the flight ma'am?" she said warmly.

"It was very comfortable. Well, after you know…"

"Oh, I understand and how many do you need for the return flight?" Margo asked, lifting her perfectly arched eyebrow.

"I need whatever you can stand to part with," I said greedily with my hand outstretched. I knew this shit was going to cost me but I didn't care. I hadn't slept that well in over a month and I needed those pills to help me through this whole ordeal.

"Meet me in the bathroom. I don't want anyone to see us," she said and stepped around me and went inside the woman's room.

I took a deep breath and followed behind her. I

signaled to Katavious to let him know I was headed to the rest room and he waved me along. I had no idea what the hell I was about to do, but I prayed like hell I wasn't walking into trouble following behind some pill-pushing flight attendant.

When we got in the bathroom she checked under the handicapped stall and took me by the hand and pulled me inside.

"What is that you gave me?" I asked as soon as she had closed and locked the door.

She pulled a baggie full of the green pills out of her apron. My eyes lit up.

"They are nothing but muscle relaxers. They make you sleep. That's why you were out the whole flight. Plus, you had those drinks they amped up the affect. I charge twenty a pill. Are you game, because I don't have much time before I have to board my next flight," Margo said looking at her watch.

I fished around in my bra and pulled out ten twenty dollar bills and handed them to Margo. She handed me the entire bag and walked out the stall.

"Oh, and honey watch how much alcohol you drink with those things," she warned and sashayed out of the restroom.

I stuffed the plastic bag in my waistband and exited out and made my way over to Katavious who was standing by the baggage claim with an annoyed look on his face. I ignored him and took my rolling luggage from him. I was not going to let him get under my skin. The fact of the matter is that he needed me. He could hate me all he wanted.

Katavious brushed past me and headed to pick up the car from the rental place.

I don't know what came over me, but I was happy to be far away from DC and all the things that troubled me there. I sat browsing the tourist guides while Katavious got the car. I stuffed one of the brochures in my bag, hoping that I would be able to get away and see some of the sights. There was no way I had come all of this way not to see anything.

Katavious motioned for me to follow him. His aggressive behavior was rubbing me the wrong way and I was sick of it. I was scared of him, but not afraid enough to not speak on it.

Once we were in the confines of the car, I addressed him because I wasn't going to be able to make it the entire time we had to deal with one another like this.

"Katavious, I know you don't like me, and I don't know why you don't fuck with me, but we have a job to do. Our job is to act like we like one another or we will fuck around and wind up in handcuffs. I don't know about you, but I don't want to go to jail. I just want to do what we came here to do and go home and finish it. I don't want to be a thorn in your side no longer than you want to be one in mine," I said, trying to be as friendly as I possibly could.

Katavious acted like he hadn't heard a word I had said to him. He turned up the radio and ignored me the entire trip to the hotel. I sat saying nothing else to him. I watched the beautiful land unfold before me. I can't say there was much difference between DC and Lagos.

It was a grand city. The entire place was surrounded by water. There were majestic buildings and the trees reminded me of palm trees. The one thing I noticed was the intense heat. I wasn't prepared for it and it was something I could truly do without.

I was amazed that we had pulled up at the Four Points by Sheraton. I guess everything I thought I knew about Africa was shattered. Everyone was hustling about on their cell phones and doing the same things we did in the States. I was truly in awe of what I had seen thus far. We entered the hotel and I instantly tensed up. I have never thought about our sleeping and living arrangements until right then. I hope that Adekite had made arrangements for me to have my own room because it was hard enough living in the same city as Katavious. There was no way I was going to stay in a hotel for any amount of time with him.

We made our way to the desk and I was relieved when he checked in and got a two-bedroom suite. I started to object and get my own room that was far away from him, but I didn't think testing Katavious right now was a very good idea. This situation was already intense and I don't think he would have appreciated me protesting about the room and me not wanting to be in it with him.

Katavious used his keycard in the elevator and we were whisked to the tenth floor. When the elevator doors opened it gave way to a huge penthouse. The entire mini apartment was glass. I could see clear to the ocean from where our room was positioned. The view was breathtaking. Katavious didn't seem to care about any of it and tossed his bags on the leather couch and walked up to me.

"This is your keycard to get in and out of the room. Make sure when you come and go no one is with you because we ain't here to make friends. We are here to make money. You got that?" He said, shoving the card in my hand.

I rolled my eyes and nodded my head. I still felt a little woozy from the muscle relaxer and didn't feel like any confrontation with Katavious.

"Good. I would hate to make you come up missing. I don't feel like explaining to my brother why you never made it back to America. Unlike me, he gives a fuck about you making it back to America. I, on the other hand, could care less. Just stay out of my way while we are here and do as I tell you or you won't make it back to DC!" Katavious growled and got back in the elevator and left.

I don't think I exhaled until he had left and I was sure that he wasn't coming back. I couldn't help but think this man may have been the person who called me before we left the States. He seemed to hate me and had very little reason to. I had never spoken more than ten words to him at any one sitting.

This was going to be the longest three days of my life. I took my bags into my part of the suite and made sure to lock the door behind me. I didn't take Katavious threats lightly. He seemed to hate me so much that he would make good on me never returning home. I went through my purse and found the brochure I had picked up at the airport and felt like going out to see what Nigeria was all about. I wasn't a fan of the extreme heat, but I couldn't see flying all this way and see nothing.

There was a day trip and I wanted to check on it. I took the elevator down to the lobby and asked the clerk about the sight-seeing tours. She let me know there was one tourist bus that picked up guests once a day and I had just missed it. She made it a point to tell me about all of the activities the hotel offered. None of it seemed to interest me until she pointed me in the direction of the bar. I thanked her and decided if I was stuck at the hotel then I would rather do it drunk. I pulled up a seat at the bar and made myself comfortable. The bartender, whose skin was as dark as night, took my order. I made sure to let him know to keep them coming and to charge all of it to my room. I figured if I had to be here, then I was going to get something out of it for free. I stayed at the bar until I was pissy drunk and there was nothing left for me to do but go back to my room.

I stumbled trying to make it through the hotel lobby. I struggled to walk straight, but finally gave up and took off the six inch *Manolos* and tried my hardest to get to the elevator without landing on my face. I was grateful that the elevator didn't take long. There were too many people around and I am sure I was making a complete fool of myself. I knew Adekite wouldn't be too happy to know about my behavior. I made it to the room safely and passed out on the sofa until late the next morning.

WWW.GSTREETCHRONICLES.COM

On The Run

hen I woke up the following morning it took me a minute to remember where I was and what I was doing in my strange surroundings. The reality of where I was flooded my thoughts. I slowly started to remember that I had flown to Africa to make a drug trade for Adekite with his asshole brother, Katavious. As soon as I thought about Katavious, I shot straight up on the couch and looked around the room nervously. There was no sign of him. I tiptoed through the suite to see if he had come in. When I didn't see him, and his room door was wide open, I decided to take a look inside. The first thing I noticed was that his luggage was in the same spot he had left it the day before, indicating that he had not come back to the room since he had left earlier the previous day. All of his identification was on the dresser along with his plane ticket back to America. I focused my sights on the big black suitcase Katavious had totted with him.

My curiosity got the better of me and I had to see

what was inside that bag. I walked over to the bag and my palms got slick with sweat. I unzipped the bag and inside was rows upon rows of hundred dollar bills bound together by bank tape. Each stack of hundreds was marked and the markers around each stack read, "$10,000."

I didn't know how many stacks of hundreds were in that bag and I didn't care. I can't explain what happened next or why I did it. Maybe greed motivated me to do it, but I raced around the room and gathered all of Katavious's travel documents and shoved them in the bag with the money and closed the bag. I pulled the bag along with me to my room and called the front desk.

"Yes, ma'am, this is Samantha Underwood in the penthouse suite. Can you please call a cab for me and send someone to get my luggage. I am going to be checking out earlier than I expected."

The woman agreed and said that the bell hop would be there in a few minutes. I hung up and moved my luggage that I hadn't unpacked near the elevator. I slid on my flat shoes, put on my sun glasses, and nearly jumped out of my skin when the elevator chimed letting me know someone was there. I almost ran and hid until I saw the bell hop making his way off the elevator and gathering my things.

He must have seen the panic on my face. "Madam your taxi is waiting for you downstairs. I came to help you take your things down." The man explained.

I nodded my head in his direction and quickly got myself under control. I knew what I was doing was dead wrong and had me all jumpy. I walked to the elevator and prayed that Katavious wouldn't come in before I could make my escape. I only had one chance to do this shit and I had to do it right. I was in a strange country that I know nothing about, with a bag full of money that belonged to a drug lord that I was now stealing. The ride down on the elevator felt like an eternity. I had to will myself to walk across the lobby calmly, instead of making a break for it like I wanted to. The bell hop led me to the taxi that was waiting out front. He loaded my luggage in the trunk and I got inside. I gave the man a crisp hundred dollar bill and thanked him for his help.

"Where to ma'am?" The cabbie asked in his thick accent.

"The airport and make it quick please. I have a plane to catch. If you can get me there in under twenty minutes there is something in it for you," I said trying to make the cabbie understand that I needed to get to the airport in a hurry.

The man didn't say anything else to me and pulled away just as Katavious pulled up in the rental car. I slouched down in the seat so he couldn't see me. My heart thundered wildly in my chest and my face was slick with sweat. I knew he had seen me. I knew I had been caught. I closed my eyes because I didn't want to see Katavious follow me because I knew once he caught up to me, I was a dead woman. There was no talking my way out of this and I knew he wasn't going to want to hear any excuse I could have possibly given him as to why I taken his brother's money and ran. I didn't open my eyes until I heard the cabbie talking to me.

"Ma'am, your fare is five Kobo."

I didn't know what the hell he was talking about. I gave him a hundred dollar bill and hoped that was enough to cover my fare. He snatched the bill out of my hands greedily and smiled his toothless smile. I figured I had given him more than the fare plus one hell of a tip. I looked out the back window. I didn't see Katavious like I thought I would and breathed a sigh of relief.

I got out and the cabbie followed me with my bags to the information desk. I needed to switch my flight and get out of Nigeria before Katavious had figured out that I had robbed him and was about to flee the country with the money that was supposed to be for the exchange of his brother's drugs.

The woman at the counter told me I was in luck and that a flight would be leaving for the United States in thirty minutes and they had had a cancellation. The only downfall was that the flight was headed to the one place I would rather not go, Washington, DC. I didn't have much choice but to get the first flight out and then worry about how I was going to relocate after that. The last thing I wanted was to get off the plane and be met by a pissed off Adekite.

I paid the woman for my ticket and gave the woman my passport. After she checked me in for my flight, I took a seat in a secluded spot near the boarding gate and opened the big black bag that the money was in. I stuffed a few of the bundles in my own carry-on and closed the bag up hoping no one saw the contents inside. I then went back to the desk and asked the clerk to please check the bag. I wasn't comfortable having to go back through customs in DC with that amount of money. Especially since I wasn't going to have the protection of whoever was working for Adekite at the TSA.

I boarded my flight twenty minutes later. I settled in for the nineteen-hour flight and found the muscle relaxers I had bought from Margo. I ordered two shots of Remy Martin as soon as the flight attendant started making her way down the aisle. Once I paid for my drinks, I took two of the pills and downed both of the shots. The liquor burned my throat, but I knew that burn was going to be short lived. Not even thirty minutes later, my lids grew heavy and I was fast asleep flying high over the Atlantic Ocean.

I dreamt that I made it all the way back home to America safely with the money in my hands. I would make a fresh new start far away from DC and Adekite, Katavious, Marshall's mother, and Shaunie. They would never know where to find me because I had no idea as to where I was going to run away too.

My dream fast forwarded, and I was in a sunny place. I stood on the balcony while the morning sun kissed my tanned cheeks. I felt good and I felt free. I was enjoying the bright sunshine beaming down on me when I saw Katavious watching me from the ground below. I backed into the sliding glass door and looked around the room frantically for anything to protect myself with. I crept over to the phone and tried to dial 911. Before I could punch in the numbers, the door came crashing in and Adekite was standing there with a twisted grin on his face. He held up a gun with a silencer attached to it. I knew I was going to die. Adekite had found me and he was going to kill me for taking his money. Katavious and Ohruh joined their brother.

Ohruh took the gun from Adekite's hands and pointed it in my direction. I shook my head no. Out of the three brothers, I thought he would be the one I could talk some sense into. I tried to open my mouth to speak and he pulled the trigger.

I woke up with tears streaming from my big blue eyes. I rubbed my eyes and saw the familiar landscape unfold before me. The plane had touched down at BWI Airport. I was happy to know that it was all a dream and that Ohruh hadn't really pulled the trigger. I sat there thanking God for my safe return back to the States. Once we were off the plane and through customs I felt relieved. I hurried along to baggage claim to get my luggage. I stood there waiting until the carousel started to spin and the bags started to appear. I retrieved my first bag and waited impatiently for the second bag with the money to come out. I waited there for an hour. People came and went and there was still no bag. I stormed over to the information desk and I asked the clerk was there anything else from the flight that was supposed to be unloaded. When she told me no, I all but lost it. I reached over the counter and threatened the clerk's life. The young woman was apologetic for the mix up and kept asking me to fill out a missing luggage form. I pointed my acrylic nail in her face and demanded that she get up off her narrow ass and find my bag. The young woman was stunned at my behavior and set off the silent alarm alerting airport security that she was in need of help.

Within moments, I was surrounded by airport personnel who dragged me from the counter; kicking and screaming. They weren't trying to hear anything about my lost bags. They wanted me out of their airport and threatened to call the police on me if I didn't leave quietly. I gave up when I heard them mention the cops and left the airport defeated.

There was no doubt in my mind that Adekite and Katavious would be looking for me and their money; money that I no longer had because it had been lost or stolen within the airport.

I calmed down long enough so that they would just let me leave alone without calling the authorities on me. I didn't need any more cops on my ass. I had not too long ago got them off my ass for Marshall's death.

I straightened up my clothes and walked out the airport and headed straight for the garage to collect my car. My mind was swimming. I was feeling all kinds of emotions rolled into one. I was anxious to get away, but I knew I had to go back to the house and get my shit so I could go. My original plan was to just leave DC with the money and worry about my possessions later. With the type of money I thought I had, I could have bought all new shit. There was no way I was going to be able to do that now being that my money was lost somewhere between here and Africa and I had no real claims to the luggage either. All of Katavious' identification was in the luggage so even if it turned up the airport authorities would most likely return the lost bag to Katavious and Adekite. That's *if* they return it. Knowing those thieving ass mother fucka's they would keep the shit for themselves.

I cranked up the car and headed to the house. I needed to get whatever I could get and be out. I probably didn't have much time before Adekite and Katavious would come looking for me. I knew at best Katavious was stuck in Lagos with no travel documents to get back. That was only a delay. Adekite had reach across the Atlantic Ocean and I am sure he would figure out a way to get Katavious back home to DC, and when he did, I had better be gone because he wasn't going to take me stealing from him too lightly.

CHAPTER SIXTEEN

Shit Just Got Real

I pulled the truck into the driveway and killed the engine. I looked around making sure I was alone because anyone could have been lying in wait, watching for me to slip up. I ran at full speed from the truck to the house. I was moving so fast I barely closed the door to the truck in my attempt to make it to the house unharmed. I fumbled with the keys. My hands were shaking so bad I could barely get the key in the lock. When I finally got in the door, I slammed it shut and took the stairs two at a time. I stopped at the threshold of the master bedroom. My entire bedroom was in an uproar. Everything was thrown all about.

I backed away from the room, afraid someone might still be in the house. I tried not to make a sound as I crept back down the steps. I had almost made it to the front door when in walked Tieriek. I had almost forgotten about him. I fell into his arms, grateful that he had shown up when he did.

"What are you doing here?" I asked him. I held onto

him like my life depended on it.

"I got a call over the radio about a disturbance. Imagine my surprise when I saw it was your address. Is everything ok? Are you alright?" Tieriek asked me.

"I think someone is in my house. They totally trashed the master bedroom," I said between sobs.

Tieriek headed for the stairs and I followed right behind him. I didn't want to be left alone in fear that whoever had fucked up my bedroom could still be in the house. When we made it to the second floor he checked each room. Once he was confident that no one was on the upper level of the house, we proceeded to check the lower level. Whoever had been there was long gone now. I begged Tieriek not to report what had happened. I didn't need any more cops snooping around the house and making my shit hotter than it already was. All I wanted was to get what I could and get ghost before whoever had been there returned.

"I don't understand why you don't want to report any of this. Someone broke into your home and trashed it and you don't want to do anything about it?" Tieriek asked me obviously confused.

I pulled from his embrace and wiped at my tears. I had to think fast. I had to make up something to tell him. I couldn't tell him the truth. What was I going to say? That would be one hell of an explanation. *Officer, I don't know who trashed my house. I am twisted up in some ill shit. It could have been anyone looking for me. It could have been my ex's friends and family. They might be after me for killing his dumb ass. Or it could be the Nigerian drug lord who I robbed in Nigeria before flying back to the U.S.*

I could see his face now if I had told him the truth, and that was only a piece of the truth. The real truth was that I had burned more than just a few people. Anyone could have it out for me. I had done my fair share of dirt and anyone could have wanted my head at this point.

"Look, Tieriek, I know none of this looks good, but I don't want to report any of this. I told you Marshall was a mess and there is no telling who he pissed off before he died. For all I know, he could have owed someone money and they broke in here looking for it. I just want to get what I can and leave before they come back," I said, sobbing quietly.

"Well, why don't you let me get an officer to at least watch the house for you. That way if someone comes back, then we can have them brought in for questioning."

I shook my head no. I knew he was just trying to help, but the only way he could help me was to wait while I packed up my shit and got out of there. I didn't know how much time I had and I was wasting it sitting here while Tieriek tried to give me alternative options that I wasn't interested in.

Suddenly, Tieriek snapped his fingers. "That reminds me, you know that plate number you gave me?" he asked.

I shrugged my shoulders. I didn't know what the hell he was talking about.

"You know...the tag number of your boyfriend's partner?" He said, reminding me that I had given him Marshall's mother's tag number to buy me some time to find somewhere else to live.

"Yes, I remember now. What about her?"

"We picked her up yesterday afternoon. She keeps claiming she knows nothing about moving drugs and when we mentioned Marshall to her, she broke down and started crying. The crazy woman said that he was her son and that she was not involved in any illegal activities. We have been holding her until we can either get her to confess or you can ID her as being Marshall's connect."

I smiled. That's just what I wanted to hear...that they had that old bag locked up somewhere. Then it dawned on me; if she was locked up, then that meant it definitely wasn't her that had torn through my home. My fear that had subsided temporarily knowing that she was locked up, had returned.

"What will I have to do to ID her? I won't have to go to court or anything; will I? I can't get mixed up in Marshall's shit!" I said nervously.

Tieriek took my hands in his. "No, Samantha. You identifying her will be totally confidential. It will be just like those lineups you see on television. We will place you in a room where the suspects can't see you, but you can see them and then you point them out. Do you think you can do that?"

"Yes...yes. I can do it. Will you be there with me? I don't think I can do it alone," I said, batting my long lashes at him seductively.

"I will be wherever you need me to be pretty lady," Tieriek said.

Tieriek waited with me while I made several trips back and forth from the house to the car with my belongings. I took everything that I could move out of the house that didn't require a mover. When I was finished Tieriek escorted me to place the bigger things in a storage unit. I agreed to call him once I got myself settled. I told him a little white lie and said that I would be staying with friends until I could find somewhere else to live. I didn't want him to think I didn't have anywhere to go besides a hotel.

I would be telling a lie if I said I wasn't sad about having to move from my home. I had just gotten used to the idea that I had a place of my own. I drove through DC wondering what my next move was going to be. I truly had no idea. I had stolen money from Adekite on a whim, and before I had the chance to relocate to someplace warm and sunny, the money was stolen from me.

Karma was a bitch.

I calculated the money that I had left from what Adekite had given me as an advance and the amount I had transferred from the suitcase back in the Nigerian hotel, to be close to an easy forty grand. My greed made me want to kick myself for not taking the entire stash of Adekite's money and transferring it to my own bags.

Easy come easy go. I thought while I travelled around with no real destination. I thought about going to lay low at my parent's house, but decided against it. Although no one would look for me in the hood, I would have to worry about them robbing me blind or begging me for anything they thought I might have. I also didn't want to run the risk of bumping into Nee Nee. Since she and I were on less than favorable terms there was no telling what she might try to do. She could possibly know about the money I took from Adekite and sell me out. After all, Adekite, Rasaun and Marshall were all working together.

My best bet was to lay low and steer clear of anyone who may be my enemy. While I drove around aimlessly trying to figure out what my next move was going to be, my cell phone started to ring. My phone hadn't made a peep the entire time I had been gone. I thought about it more and more and I realized that it hadn't rung since the night I stayed in the hotel before I left for Nigeria. I looked at the screen and the screen read, *no caller information*, which meant whoever was calling was blocking their number. I cautiously answered the phone. "Hello."

There was silence on the other end.

I was in no mood to play the *hello* game with whoever was on the other end. I knew someone was there because I could hear them breathing. I hung up quickly because if they weren't going to announce themselves then neither was I. No sooner than I had thrown the phone in the passenger seat of the truck when the phone started to ring again. I picked it up and again, it displayed, *no caller information,* again.

"Look, I don't know who this is or what you want, but you need to stop calling my phone and not announcing yourself." I screamed into the phone.

"You stupid white bitch, I told you not to fuck with me. Where is my money? Better yet where are you with my money so I can cut your head off and deliver it to your junkie parents? You better start running because if I catch you, you're dead!"

I suddenly became very aware of who the caller was. It was Adekite. I swallowed the large lump that had formed in my throat. I thought about telling him that I had been robbed, but I knew he wouldn't believe me. I knew no matter what I said to him, he wasn't trying to hear it unless I was telling him where his money was.

"Bitch, did you hear me? You better start talking!" Adekite growled into the phone.

I did the only thing I could do, I hung up. I was so shaken I wasn't paying attention to the road and kissed the bumper of the car in front of me.

"Fuck!" I screamed. I threw the truck in park, unfastened my seatbelt and hopped out of the truck. I had better put on one hell of a show because I knew damn well I didn't have insurance. I let that shit lapse when Marshall died.

The driver of the car got out and I could tell she was mad as hell. I did a double take when the driver got closer. I couldn't believe my luck. It was Marshall's old flame, Erica. When she realized who I was she smiled a wicked smile. Her face was burned from the scalding water I had thrown on her a few months back. I thought she was going to come after me. Instead, she turned around and ran full speed to her car. She was screaming at the top of her lungs.

"Oh, you wait right there bitch, I got something for your ass!" Erica yelled.

I was in a state of shock. My feet felt like they were glued to the pavement. I watched in horror as Kendra reached inside her car door, which was still wide open, and pulled out the steering wheel club. I didn't get my ass in gear fast enough. Kendra came at me fast, swinging the steering wheel lock. I don't know why I didn't start moving before she charged me. I started to turn a second too late. I felt the club make contact with my ribs, nearly knocking the wind out of me. I doubled over in pain from the heavy metal object she was battering my ribcage with.

The pain was so horrendous I dropped to my knees howling. Erica was standing over me now. She had tossed the steering wheel lock to the side. She started to stomp and kick me in the middle of the street. I couldn't understand why no one had come to my rescue. I didn't know why no one would stop her. We were in broad daylight in the middle of traffic which had totally stopped behind us and was moving at a snail's pace on the opposite side of the street.

The way the drivers of the other cars were reacting, you would have thought they would have done something about the way Erica was working me over. Instead, they just watched like my battle with this angry woman was a spectator's sport.

Erica delivered another minding blowing kick to my back which made me fall forward. My face smacked the concrete. The last thing I remembered was the sound of a horn honking and the sirens wailing somewhere in the distance before I passed out in the middle of the busy street.

Down But Not Out

When I came to, I looked around afraid that
Erica would be right there ready to deliver
another attack. She wasn't. Instead, I was alone. It took
me a moment before I realized I was in a hospital. I
pressed the button for the nurse. I wanted to know how
long I had been there. Several minutes went by before a
small-framed woman entered my room wearing scrubs.

"I see we are finally awake. You had us worried there
for a while." The woman smiled.

"My name is Shetara, and I have been your nurse for
the last three days," the woman said in a deep southern
drawl. Her words were drawn out and it was the equiv-
alent of someone scratching their nails across a chalk
board. It was annoying.

I rolled my eyes up at the ceiling because she was just
a little too chipper for me. Anyone who was this happy
outside of getting and spending money was suspect.

"What can I do for you, Ms. Underwood?"

"Where are my things and how did I get here?" I

asked wincing in pain.

"Your things are in the closet over there and you were brought in by way of an ambulance. There was a gentleman caller who kept calling to check on you. He must be really concerned about you," she continued. Her words were dragging and I wanted her to shut up, but she had said someone had called to check on me. I didn't know who that could have been, but I needed to find out.

"Shetara, did the person who called leave a message? Did he leave a name?"

She stopped taking the reading from the blood pressure cuff she had attached to my arm. She looked like she was trying to remember who had called and I was growing more and more annoyed with every second that passed. I sat there wishing I could shake her so she would remember who the message was from.

"No, ma'am. I can't recall if he left a name. There was so much going on when you first got here and we have had so many patients on this floor I can't remember if he said his name or not. I do know he called several times though," Shetara said, going about her business and writing information on what I assumed was my chart.

I swear if it wasn't for bad luck I would have no luck at all. Not only had Adekite found out I took his money, but I fucked around and got robbed for the same money I had just stolen. Of all people for me to run into...I literally ran into Erica in the street and she was on some *get back* shit. Now I had to deal with this silly nurse who couldn't remember anything.

I plastered a fake grin on my face even though it hurt. I could only imagine what my face looked like. I knew I had taken an ass whipping. If Kendra could have killed me then, she would have.

"Shetara, can you do me a favor and get my things?" I said as nicely as I could. I wanted to stay on her good side. She was so clueless she wouldn't even know I was using her dumb ass. She got the big plastic bag from the closet that had all of my clothes and my purse that someone must have taken from the truck. Thoughts of where the truck might have been ran through my mind. Now I was without a mode of transportation. I didn't know if the police had the truck towed or not, and I wasn't going to call around making myself hot trying to find out either.

I dug around through the bag and hoped like hell my purse was somewhere inside and no one had taken the cash I had left. I didn't breathe until I saw the first bundle. When I didn't feel anything but that one stack of bills that I had pushed deep down into a side pocket, I started to panic and dumped the rest of the contents on the bed. Shetara stopped writing on my chart and looked at me curiously.

"Who the fuck went in my bag?" I said, trying to control my temper; although I had to admit I was doing a piss poor job of it. I gritted my teeth trying to ignore the pain from my injuries.

"Ma'am, I really don't know. I do know they most likely got your identification out of your belongings. That's how we were able to find out your name. Why, is everything ok?"

"Does everything look ok? Fuck no! Everything ain't ok. Someone took my money from my purse!" I sobbed.

"What kind of games are ya'll playing around here?" I yelled. If I could have gotten out of that bed I would have. I wanted to spit on this stupid woman.

"Ma'am, I can assure you I don't know anything about your money or who may have taken it," Nurse Shetara said. Her face told me she was afraid and she had every right to be afraid. If I found out she had anything to do with the disappearance of my cash I was going to whip her ass.

I pressed the call button repeatedly. I wanted someone to explain where the hell my money had disappeared to. I felt like I was going insane.

Nurse Shetara continued to plead her case when a young man, who had more sugar in his tank than needed, walked in.

"Ma'am, my name is Nurse Brian Raines. I am the charge nurse. Is there something I can assist you with that Nurse Shetara could not help you with?" He asked, clearly annoyed with being called into the room where someone else was already assisting me.

"I want to know who went through my shit! That's what you can assist me with!" I demanded. I turned Samantha on and I knew I was going have to turn her all the way up if I was going to get what I wanted out of this situation – which was information.

"The paramedics went through your things. Would you like to explain what you were doing with these pills that weren't in a prescription bottle?" he said with a snotty attitude. "Or maybe we should let the police know you were in possession of an unidentified substance. The choice is up to you," he said, dangling the bag of muscle relaxers I had purchased from the flight attendant.

Nothing I had done seemed to go right. I was getting caught left and right. This cocky bastard was basically all but saying he had gone through my purse and took the money. He smirked at me. I lay back down in the bed defeated. I know I didn't want anyone to call the police for some bogus ass muscle relaxers. As soon as I thought about police, Tieriek popped up in my head. I found my cell phone and found it was dead. The charger was most likely in the truck with the rest of my shit that I knew I couldn't recover because it was uninsured and it wasn't even in my name.

The nurse, with too much milk in his shake, gave nurse Shetara a nod and left the room. Shetara looked at me apologetically.

"Ma'am, I don't know what's going on, but I will try to help you anyway I can," she offered.

"I need a cell phone charger. Can you do that for me?" I asked smugly.

"I can loan you mine. Do you need anything else?"

I wanted to tell her I wanted my life back to normal. Instead, I shook my head no and then she left the room quickly. I bet she was grateful to get away from me even if it was for only a moment. The feeling was mutual because I wasn't in any mood to hear anymore bullshit about what happened to my stuff.

I stared up at the ceiling wondering what I was going to do now. Better yet, I wondered who knew I was there and how long I was going to have to stay there. I had better enjoy my stay in the hospital because I didn't have anywhere else to go. I had better figure out something and I had better do it quick. I knew they were only going to keep me in the hospital for so long.

I laid there thinking and the pain from my injuries made me very aware of where I was. Shetara returned to my room and let me borrow her charger. I groaned in pain as I tried to plug it up.

"Ms. Underwood, do you need something for pain? I can get you a pain killer," she said, rushing to my side to assist me.

"Yes. I guess I could use something. By the way did anyone say anything about the person who did this to me? Did they at least lock her up?" I asked powering on my phone.

Immediately text messages popped up. There were thirty-seven of them in all. Thirty-two of them were from Adekite, and the rest were from Tieriek. I deleted all of Adekite's messages without reading them because I was sure what they said. He wasn't doing anything but telling me how many ways I was going to die 'if' he caught up to me. The only person I had intended on contacting was Tieriek. He might be able to help me find the truck and recover some of my belongings. He was a cop. If nothing else, he could do my snooping for me.

I sent him a message letting him know where I was and what had happened. I let him know I would be changing my number and to expect a text from me with the new one. I also asked him about my truck. I needed him to get my truck because I needed to be able to get the fuck out of DC before Adekite and Katavious found me. I needed to get as many miles between us as I could. I didn't know which way I was going, but I was determined to get there.

Shetara walked in with a cup of water and two pills. I popped them and waited for them to kick in. I wanted them to kick in fast. Thinking about the shit going on was making me think too much and I didn't want to think about anything at all. I just wanted to sleep.

"Ma'am, can I get you anything else?" Shetara slurred in that dumb accent. I wanted her to shut the fuck up and leave me alone until I really needed her. Her voice was making me cringe, but I didn't want to scare the bitch. I might need her to get me out of here if Tieriek couldn't locate my damn truck.

"No, I don't need anything else. Thank you," I said between gritted teeth and I rolled over and tried to focus on the television. Twenty minutes later I fell asleep.

I woke up eight hours later and felt better than I had felt over the last few days. I was still sore as hell from the ass whooping Kendra had put on me, but I knew they weren't going to keep me in the hospital too long over some bumps and bruises. I looked worse than I really was.

The best part about being in the hospital was that they would give me pills for the pain. They didn't care if you needed them or not. Every time I pushed the call button, Shetara came running with a cup of water and the pills and that's what I did while I was there until two days later when Shetara walked in and told me I was being discharged.

This was the day I had dreaded because Tieriek couldn't locate my truck. That meant I didn't have a way to get the fuck out of here when I was discharged.

"Ms. Underwood, is someone coming to pick you up or do you need for us to call you a cab? The doctor will be in shortly to give you your home care instructions and you will be free to go. I'm sure you will be happy to get out of here."

I don't know what made me open up and start talking to her. It wasn't like I wanted a friend or anything. I figured that if she felt sorry enough for me she would help me.

"Shetara, the truth is that money that was stolen from my purse was the money I had saved up to move. Now that the money is gone, and I can't find my truck, I have no idea where I am going to go or what I am going to do," I sniffled, hoping to make her sympathize with me.

"Oh, wow. I didn't know that. Is there anything I can do to help you?" Shetara offered.

I perked up because I knew I had her right where I wanted her.

"I know I wasn't very nice in the beginning, but I really need a place to stay until the police find my truck. Do you think you can help me out?" I asked sheepishly. I knew it was a long shot but what other choice did I really have?

Shetara closed the door behind her. "What about

your family? Don't you have anyone?" She asked full of sorrow.

I shook my head no. I did everything I could to seem like a damsel in distress.

"Ma'am, it is highly unethical for us to do this with patients. If you need some place to stay I have a spare bedroom in my house. It isn't much, but you are more than welcome to it until you can locate your truck, but you have to promise not to tell anyone what I am doing for you because it could cost me my job."

I wiped at the big crocodile tears and had to stop myself from smiling. This was easier than I thought it would be.

"Shetara, I don't know how to thank you. I promise I won't be in your way and I will be gone before you know it and I swear I won't tell anyone anything about this. This is embarrassing enough that I have to beg for a place to stay."

"Well, I am glad I am able to help! My shift ends in a few minutes. The doctor should have discharged you by then and we can leave together," Shetara beamed.

I was glad she was receptive of the idea because she didn't know I was leaving this hospital with her no matter how she felt about it. I gathered my things and patiently waited for Shetara to finish her shift. I got my prescriptions from the doctor and we left the hospital with me looking over my shoulder the entire way.

CHAPTER EIGHTEEN

Drastic Times Call For Drastic Measures

We pulled up to Shetara's two-bedroom row house in N.W. Washington DC. I wasn't impressed. I did everything I could to hide my displeasure for being in the city, and most of all having to be there with her. I found out very fast that she was nosey and even more irritating than I first thought. It was more than her voice that was getting on my nerves. It was just about everything about her; but what choice did I have in the matter? I needed a place to lay low and she was the only person willing to let me crash at her place. The entire ride to her piece of a home she asked question after question about me and my family. I had lied so much to her about who I really was, that I couldn't keep up anymore. I was saying just about anything to keep her out of my face.

I eased out of the car and made sure no one was watching me. I knew I stuck out like a sore thumb in this neighborhood. I was the only white woman here. There was nothing but snotty nose kids running around being destructive, and their welfare mothers weren't doing anything but allowing them to run around like gutter trash. The niggas were on the block trying to make enough money so they could floss. It was your typical hood setting.

It wasn't that I wasn't used to seeing shit like this, because I grew up in it; but I didn't want to see any of it because I had had enough of seeing this shit my entire life. I couldn't figure out what a nurse was doing living in a neighborhood like this. If I had a job like that, there was no way I would be living in the lap of poverty.

When we entered Shetara's home, the inside was totally different from the outside. Her home was fully furnished and it was neat and upscale. Shetara showed me around her place and gave me permission to help myself to whatever I needed. All I wanted her to do was leave me alone so I could concentrate on getting my plan of action in order.

When she led me to the room where I would be staying, I turned my nose up at the sight of the small twin bed. It was a far cry from the California King Size bed I had left behind at Marshall's house.

As soon as thoughts of Marshall entered my mind, my cell phone started to buzz in my pocket. I knew it was no one but Tieriek because no one had the new number since I had changed it to keep Adekite from calling me.

"Hey, beautiful! I was just checking in on you. Is everything ok?" Tieriek said.

"I guess. I hope you got some information on my truck. I really don't know how long I'm going to be able to survive without my vehicle." I sighed into the phone.

POWDER

"Actually, that is one of the reasons I was calling you. I got good news and I got some not so good news. The good news is I was able to locate the truck. The bad news is that you are going to have to bring proof of insurance and your registration to the impound lot to pick it up along with six hundred dollars," Tieriek said as if I were supposed to be able to magically make that happen.

"Tieriek, I don't have the money to get the truck." I lied. I wasn't going to spend one penny on getting that truck out of impound. I had the money to get the truck but I had other things to do with what little money I had left. Tieriek had no idea I had the money and I wasn't going to offer him that information. Besides, I still had the problem of not being able to produce any documents that legally stated that the vehicle was mine. I definitely wasn't going to tell him that because it wasn't any of his business.

"Well, let me see what I can do. Maybe I can call in a few favors and have them release the truck to you. I may be able to pull a few strings and get them to release it to me. Don't get your hopes up, but I will see what I can get done. Oh, and when will you be able to come to the station so we can take care of the business with Marshall's partner? I can't hold her here forever and her lawyers are bonding her out. She claims that this was all a mistake and that your ex, Marshall was her son, not her business partner. Do you know anything about that?"

Oh, shit! I had all but forgotten about Marshall's mother's nosey ass. I didn't even give the fact that she had been locked up a second thought. I only wanted her out of my way until I could get out of that house for good.

"Tieriek what will happen to her if she bonds out?" I asked not really caring what happened to the old bag.

"They will drop the charges against her if I can't produce a witness who can tie her to his death."

I stood there thinking about how I could care less what happened to her. I felt a migraine coming on strong and wanted to go to the pharmacy and get my pain medication. That seemed to be the only thing that kept me in the right frame of mind these days. I wasn't trying to hear anything else from Tieriek until he found a way to get my truck, or at the very least, get my shit out of it.

"Tieriek, baby, I am feeling kind out of it. I think I'm going to grab something to eat, take one of my pain medications and rest for a while. It has been a long day. I will call you once I feel better," I said. I didn't even wait for him to respond, I just hung up in his ear. I didn't feel like listening to him tell me what he couldn't do. If he couldn't do what I wanted him to do then he was no good to me anyway.

I flopped down on the little bed and wondered how I was going to get myself out of this mess. I had not one, but two Nigerian drug lords on my ass, and my best friend hated me. I didn't know how I was going to get my belongings out of the truck that wasn't registered in my name from the impound lot, and that bitch, Erica, was still walking the streets like she was the Queen Bitch.

"Hey, Samantha, I thought I was going to have the night off but it looks like I have to go back to the hospital. Brian called me in to cover someone's shift. I didn't know if you needed anything or not, but I can get a ride to work with Brian and I will leave you the car so you can pick up your prescriptions," Shetara said, standing in the doorway.

For a moment I almost forgot I was in her home. I perked up when she said she would leave her car for me to drive.

"Thanks for everything Shetara. I really appreciate it. I promise I will just run to the pharmacy and I will be right back," I said. She didn't need to know I had other plans for her car.

Shetara tossed me the keys and went about her business. I sat in my borrowed bedroom contemplating what I was going to do next. I knew I was wrong as two left shoes for even thinking of what I was about to do, but I didn't have much of a choice. I went to the kitchen and waited on that asshole Brian to pick Shetara up and I prayed that his sweet ass didn't come inside because he might have tried to stop Shetara from lending me her car. I guess I didn't pray hard enough because he pulled up ten minutes later. I watched him make a dramatic exit from his car and he sashayed up the walkway. I rolled my eyes at the sight of him. He was just like every single person from my past that I had encountered – a thorn in my side!

I decided to try to play it cool with him because I didn't want him to know I was up to no good. I greeted him at the door before he had a chance to even ring the bell.

"Hello, Nurse Raines," I said, plastering a fake grin on my face.

"What are you doing here?" Brian asked totally confused about me being there.

"Oh, Shetara was nice enough to let me stay for a few days until I can recover my money you...I mean that was stolen from me," I said slyly.

"I'm going to have to talk to that girl about picking up strays. You just can't let everyone in your home!" he mumbled, rolling his neck from side to side.

I didn't have the chance to give him a piece of my mind before Shetara interrupted us. I know she could feel the tension between the two of us. She took Brian by the hand and led him out of the house to diffuse an escalating situation. I could hear him fussing and cursing at Shetara like she was a two-year-old child all the way to the car.

I waited until I knew the coast was clear, and then I darted back to the little ass room and grabbed up my belongings. I rushed down the hall and pushed open the door to Shetara's room. She had all types of trinkets and knick knacks on her dresser. I went through what appeared to be a jewelry box and cuffed a pair of earrings that I hoped were real. There were several rings and bracelets inside the box that I decided to take too. I dumped the jewelry in my purse and proceeded to go through each one of her dresser drawers hoping to find anything of value. Not once while I ransacked her belongings did I feel bad about what I was doing. That country bitch had a job; she could replace anything I decided to take.

Next, I went through her closet. There wasn't too much that I wanted from out of there because Shetara clearly had no taste at all. I found a few pieces of clothing that I knew would fit. I found a duffle bag on the floor of the closet and threw the clothes inside. Once I was sure I had gotten everything I could of value out of Shetara's home, I got out of there as fast as I could, afraid that she may return and catch me robbing her dumb ass blind.

I guess I was moving too fast because I got all the way to Shetara's car with her valuables stuffed in my purse and her stolen luggage when I realized I didn't have the keys to her cream colored Lexus that sat in its assigned parking space right in the front of her house.

"Fuck!" I screamed at myself and marched back up the walkway and prayed with every step that I took that I hadn't locked the door behind me when I left out.

I found the door was unlocked and thanked God for small favors and went back inside to find where I had left the keys Shetara had given me before she left with Brian. I took the stairs two at a time hoping to find them and get the hell out of there. I looked high and low and could not find where I had placed the keys. I was so distraught about finding the keys that I almost decided against what I had originally intended on doing.

"Think Powder, think!" I said aloud to myself while tearing up the bed that would have been the bed I would have been sleeping on had I not decided to rob the only person who was nice enough to give me a place to lay my head. I searched all over that room and gave up. I didn't remember taking them to Shetara's room, but I ran full speed down the hallway to check anyway. I was almost in tears until something told me to check the jewelry box I had taken her earrings and bracelets from. I lifted the top on the box and there were the keys. I must have dropped them in there when I was cuffing the jewelry.

I thanked God again for small favors and bounded down the stairs only to be met by none other than that sweet mutha' fucka' Brian Raines at the door blocking my path.

He put his hands on his frail hips and rolled his neck around and I knew this shit was not going to end well.

"Ummm hmmm. Where are you going so fast?" he said rolling his eyes.

I knew I looked guilty as sin. I could feel my face growing hot and I knew it had gone over to a shade of red. There was no hiding my guilt. My facial expression told it all.

"Brian, you scared me. I was just running to the pharmacy to pick up my prescription. I have to hurry before they close. I really don't know my way around this part of town," I said nervously. I wanted to push him out of the way and make a run for it to the car.

Brian turned his nose up like I smelled bad. "It doesn't look like you are going to the store to me. It looks like you were about to leave for good. Who takes a duffle bag to the pharmacy?" He said inching closer to me. I backed up. I didn't want him that close to me.

"I don't know what's going on with you white girl, but

I don't like it. I told Shetara she shouldn't trust your pale ass! I knew from the moment they brought you into the hospital you weren't nothing but trouble! Nawh, she ain't listen, and now I think you are up to something bitch!" he said, poking me in the chest.

"I don't know what you think is going on, but ain't shit going on here but me going to the store to handle my business. No one has time to stand here and argue with you about what I'm doing and where I'm going," I countered. I smacked his hand away from my chest and tried again to push past him.

"Won't Shetara be surprised when she finds out the very bag she sent me back here to get you were stealing?"

Like the bitch he wanted to be, he shoved me hard and sent me tumbling to the floor. I thought about fighting him back, but I had to remind myself he was a man, no matter how much of a woman he tried to be.

Brian stepped over me and walked to the living room. There was no doubt in my mind that he was going for the phone. I kicked off my shoes and scrambled to get to my feet. I ran at full speed and shoved Brain hard in the back. He went crashing down, with a sickening scream, through the huge glass coffee table that was in front of him. I pushed him so hard I almost went down with him. Regaining my balance, I got myself in a stance to fight him if need be, but he didn't move. It felt like an eternity had passed me by before I got up enough courage to inch closer and see his body was twisted and contorted. There were thick shards of glass all around Brian's body and it didn't take a genius to know that he was dead by the way his body was bent at such an odd angle.

I rushed over to his lifeless body and patted his pockets, in hopes of recovering some of my money I am sure he had stolen from me in the hospital. I found his wallet and a set of keys. I went through his wallet and removed the cash that he had tightly stuffed into the leather wallet. A bank band fell to the floor at my feet. It was the same band that had held the stacks of cash I had taken from Adekite that had turned up missing after my stay at the hospital. I put the cash in my bra and his keys in my pocket, along with his credit card and his license.

"That will teach your nosey ass to mind your own fucking business!" I said. I spit on his twisted torso, walked back towards the front door picking up the bag full of Shetara's stolen belongings and walked right out the front door.

I disarmed the alarm on Shetara's car, hopped inside and cranked up the engine. I took Brian's license from my pocket and punched in the address in the GPS system. The automated voice let me know my destination was only ten minutes away. I backed out of the parking space and headed in the direction of where the computerized voice instructed me to go. Ten minutes later, I pulled up in front of an upscale apartment complex. The GPS guided me right to Brian's front door. I pulled my hair down over my face so no one could identify me if they were asked. I fished around in my bag and found a pair of shades and put them on. I knew I had better move fast if I didn't want to get caught. I was working on borrowed time before Shetara would be looking for Brian to return back to work.

I was glad this was a nice neighborhood, unlike Shetara's. I didn't look out of place. No one paid me any attention as I walked up to Brian's door and fumbled with his keys until I found the right one. The key slide in the lock like butter and turned. I could hear my heart thundering as the bolt slid from the chamber and I turned the knob effortlessly.

The cool air hit me in the face as soon as I walked in and closed the door behind me. I marveled at all the nice shit that sugary sweet ass Brian had. If I had more time I would have taken everything I could. *He won't be using it anymore!* I thought as I began to smile.

I went straight for Brian's bedroom and did to him as I had done to Shetara and took everything I could that looked like it was worth anything. I went through his shoe boxes and found what I had come there to get, some of my money. It wasn't all of it, but I was happy to get at least some of it. I was getting real tired of losing money. It was getting harder to keep it than it was to steal it from people.

I had already started formulating my next moves in my head as I exited Brian's house.

G STREET CHRONICLES
~A LITERARY POWERHOUSE~

WWW.GSTREETCHRONICLES.COM

Plan Of Attack

I called Tieriek and made up some shit about how I needed to see him. The fact remained that I had not only robbed two people, but I had killed another man and the only place I thought I would be safe, where no one would expect me to be, was with a cop. I ditched Shetara's car a few miles away from Brian's home and flagged down a cab. I gave the cabbie the address Tieriek had given me and laid my head back in the seat, hoping that my plan would work. I only needed to stay with Tieriek until I thought the coast was clear for me board a flight undetected.

I pulled up in front of Tieriek's home and noticed that it was a lot of property for one man to live in by himself. I paid the driver, gathered my things and headed up the steps. Before I could ring the bell Tieriek opened the door and pulled me inside.

"I'm glad you're here, Samantha," he said, closing the door and pulling me into a warm embrace.

He caught me off guard and kissed my lips so tenderly

that it made my body tingle. I forgot about all the robberies and Brian's lukewarm body. Dropping my bags at my feet, I melted into Tieriek. His lips were succulent. He seemed so nurturing and it was turning me on. I stepped back from him so we could have a little space, because I knew if we didn't stop, I was going to give him what I knew he wanted. Something about being wrapped up in so much drama heightened my arousal.

"Damn, I'm happy to see you too. Hey, look...thank you for letting me crash here. I know things have been really crazy with me, and you really don't know me that well. You didn't have to do this. I really appreciate it," I said sincerely meaning it. Tieriek was really sweet. I could tell he was digging me. I had to admit it, even though he really wasn't my type and he was on the opposite end of the law than I was on, I was digging him too.

"Let me take your bags, Samantha. When you called I started dinner. I made spaghetti." Tieriek smiled reaching for my bag...Shetara's bag with her and Brian's stuff inside. I snatched it back and he looked at my funny.

He threw his hands up in the air. "I was just going to put it away for you. Sorry." He chuckled.

"Damn, Tieriek, I'm sorry. I just had someone jump me in the streets and someone went through my bag at the hospital and took all of my money from me. I guess I'm still a little rattled about that."

"I understand. Well, that's all behind you now. Are you ready to eat or do you want to freshen up first?" He said, brushing off the fact that I was treating him like he was the one who had taken my money from me.

He really had no idea I was involved in a lot more than just some random petty theft in the community hospital. That petty theft had turned into two robberies and a murder. I tried to act like none of those things were on my mind and handed Tieriek my bag and he showed me to his guestroom. I laughed a little at the thought that I had more room mates in one day than most people had in their lives. I told Tieriek I wanted to freshen up before we ate. He went to the kitchen to finish the salad and I took a hot shower. The hot water felt like heaven, it was as if it was washing my sins away.

I decided to wait until after dinner to take my pain medication because I didn't want Tieriek to think I was some kind of pill popper. Besides, I think he had other things in mind for us tonight. I slid into the jeans and tank top I had taken from Shetara's house. It reminded me that as soon as I got a chance I was going to have to spend some money, I really didn't have to spend right now, and get some clothes. The few things I took from her wasn't going to cut it. She wasn't as thick as I was so her jeans were hugging parts of my body they shouldn't have hugged quite so snugly.

After stashing my bag with my money and the items I had taken earlier in the day, I joined Tieriek in the dining room where he was placing our meal of: homemade spaghetti, fresh garden salad and garlic bread, with glasses of red wine, on the table. I smiled because he seemed like he was a genuinely nice guy. He was nothing like Adekite's crazy ass or Marshall's strung-out behind.

He was an all-around good guy from what I could tell. He seemed a little too perfect and something about that nagged me a bit, but I dismissed it. I figured the weird feelings were because I was used to dealing with men who weren't shit.

We ate dinner by candlelight and I saw Tieriek as someone I could easily fall in love with, but I knew my less-than-favorable past may not allow it. Once we finished eating, we sat in front of the television and watched old sitcoms. Tieriek was older than I was by about six years and his maturity intrigued me. He seemed to want so much out of life that it made me feel bad for dropping out of school when I did. When he spoke, he spoke with so much wisdom that I knew he had had the best of everything. We were polar opposites.

We connected all over again like we had on our first date. Tieriek let me know he had to be at work in the morning and he had to call it a night. Everything in me wanted to protest and tell him to stay and keep me company. It wasn't that I wasn't tired, because I really was. I just hated closing my eyes to the nightmares. I didn't want to be alone and I was about to let Tieriek know that I didn't want to be left alone either.

He insisted on walking me to my guestroom and as he was about to turn to go to his own room I grabbed him by the hand and pulled him close to me.

"Tieriek, how can I thank you for all of this?" I asked him with my eyes boring into him seductively.

"You don't have to thank me, Samantha. If nothing else we're friends; right? I didn't do anything more than a good friend would have done."

"I don't think people who are just friends usually feel like this towards one another." I rubbed my hand up and down his chiseled chest in a suggestive manner hoping he knew where I was going with this little game I was playing. I could sense from the growing bulge in his pants he knew exactly what I wanted to do. My hormones were at an all-time high. I hadn't been touched since I fucked Adekite on the deck of his pool. I was long overdue for some sexual satisfaction.

Tieriek got the hint and took my hand in his and instead of going in the guest room he led me to his bedroom. He laid me across his huge cherry wood bed and undressed me. He took off the basketball shorts and t-shirt he was wearing and stood at the foot of the bed and stared at me. I felt so alive lying there naked while my juices started to flow like a raging river in anticipation of what was about to go down.

"You know I wanted you since the day I laid my eyes on you; don't you?"

I positioned myself on my knees and crawled to the edge of the bed without saying a word and took his manhood into my hungry mouth. Tieriek groaned in ecstasy, threw his head back and enjoyed the gift I was giving him. I sucked and licked on every part of him until he placed his hands in my silky hair and pulled me so close to him that I had to focus on not choking on his swelling hardness.

"Agggghhhh, Samantha. Damn, baby, you are everything I need and want." Tieriek moaned as he thrust in and out of my willing mouth.

The sound of him moaning was turning me on and driving me crazy. Not being able to take the pleasure I was giving him, he gently pushed me away from him and laid me down on the bed. I eagerly awaited what I knew was going to be a sensual ride. Tieriek kissed every part of my body from my fingertips to my toes. I had never had anyone love my body the way he was making love to mine. He was going down in the books as the best mind and body fuck in history.

Tieriek lapped at my pearl so gently, my body shook with every stroke of his talented tongue. I was in sheer ecstasy and rode it like the waves of the ocean until I came. Tieriek snaked his way up my body and parted my legs with one fluid motion. My limbs felt weak. I hadn't fully recovered from the way he made me feel with his mouth. There was no doubt he was putting it down.

"That's all I want. I want to make you feel good, Samantha," he said and slid into me so deep I gasped.

I clawed and scratched at his back trying to hold on. It wasn't long before I felt that familiar feeling. I didn't think I was going to be able to hold on this time.

"Yes, baby...sssssss." I moaned as my building climax ripped through me. I gripped the sheets and tried to control the tremors that were running through my body while he continued to take me to new heights each and every time he brought me to another orgasm.

Tieriek pulled out of me and flipped me over and spread my cheeks apart and returned to where he was a perfect fit. Pulling up on my elbows, I rocked with him. I arched my back and gave him a porn star's show. I wiggled my thick ass and rubbed my slick center until Tieriek called out my name and came deep within my sugary walls.

What Comes Around Goes Around

Months had gone by and I thought less and less about leaving the area. I found myself falling madly in love with Tieriek. His good spirit and nature brought about a change in me. I hadn't heard a peep from Adekite and surprisingly enough, I hadn't heard too much about Brian's death. The only thing I was able to find out about it was through Tieriek, and that wasn't much because it wasn't in his district. The news only said that they had a suspect in custody and I wasn't too surprised when they released the suspect's identity. Shetara was being held in connection with the murder of Brian Raines. I dismissed the whole ordeal and figured Shetara was too stupid to even think I had anything to do with his death or maybe she knew there was no use in trying to finger me for his murder. Really who were they going to believe her or me?

I let my guard down. I started to live the life I felt like I deserved all along and Tieriek was giving me everything I needed. He went to work every day and brought home the money and I like it that way. He seemed to like it that way too. I was able to convince him to forget about Marshall's mother and they eventually let her go. I made up some bullshit about wanting to leave the past where it was.

Tieriek, being the kind of man that he was, swept the whole thing with her under the rug and acted as though it never happened. I kept the house clean the way he liked it, had his meals ready when he came home, and served up this pussy every way he wanted whenever he wanted it. No questions asked. My shit was going sweet.

My days were filled with sleeping, sexing and pleasing Tieriek. I knew I had him right where I wanted him and he had a special place in his heart for me. There was no denying his feelings for me because what man would take a woman into his home and take care of her, cherish her and respect her if he wasn't falling in love?

I finally told Tieriek that I wasn't concerned about getting Marshall's truck back. I just wanted anything I was able to recover that was inside. He called in those favors like he promised and I was allowed to get my things, although they were going to auction the truck off because I didn't have any legal papers on it and the real owner was dead. I didn't even care because Tieriek gave me full run of everything in his home and his car.

I took the money I took back from Brian and bought a whole new wardrobe. I had no complaints for the first time in a long time and I even thought about getting my GED. I hated feeling like I wasn't good enough and was secretly looking into taking some classes. I figured that since I wasn't doing much with my time, I could take the exam and if Tieriek asked me anything about what I was doing with my time I would think of something to tell him.

Tieriek had his head so far up in the clouds he believed I could do no wrong. I wasn't going to do anything but keep him in the dark about my recent past. I was fully prepared to take my dirty little secrets to the grave.

Everything in my new found life was perfect. I had a man that adored me and we seemed to be happy with one another. I seemed to be able to shake everything that had taunted me in the past. The neighborhood that we lived in seemed to accept me just the way I was. No one looked at me and Tieriek strange because we were an interracial couple, and no one seemed to care anything about my skin color like they had when I was living in the hood.

The only dark cloud that seemed to hang over me was that I still had nightmares. I hadn't seen or heard anything from Adekite and I didn't know if Katavious had made it back from Nigeria. I knew Katavious was going to have some issues with getting back, being that when I stole the money from him, I had taken his passport as well. There was no telling if or when he would be able to return to the States. I was almost one hundred percent certain that they would have never guessed I was still living right under their nose in the DMV, but I was. Since I changed my cell phone number the threatening calls ceased. I was able to relax, but when I closed my eyes and drifted off to sleep...that was when all the trouble would start. Past enemies would invade my dreams. It was so bad that the only way I was able to sleep was with the help of the pain medication that I was taking from when Erica assaulted me. A good stiff drink and a few of the Vicodin I constantly begged my new doctor for, were the only remedy that seemed to make me sleep without the nightmares.

Of course, I couldn't let Tieriek know I was popping pills. Somehow I didn't think he would approve of it. So I took them in privacy. As a matter of fact, I was headed to the doctors today so could make up some shit to tell the doctor so she would keep writing out those little slips allowing me to have access to what was becoming my drug of choice. I didn't see anything wrong with taking them as long as the doctor was prescribing them to me. They didn't seem like real drugs to me. They were: in no way, form, or fashion, like the shit out on the streets. There was no comparing my pills – that took away what I perceived as pain, but in reality was a guilty conscious and accompanying bad dreams – with the shit out on the streets. It wasn't like I was strung out like Marshall had been. I was nothing like my parents. They were all junkies. I wasn't a junkie. I was just getting rid of the nightmares. That's how I saw it, because that's how it was.

I had to get myself ready to drop Tieriek off at work and then I was headed to the doctors to get my refill and spend the rest of my day preparing for the surprise I had for Tieriek. I wanted to cook him his favorite meal and I had a special night planned for us. I wanted to really show him how much I appreciated him. I had my day fully planned. I was scheduled to go to the salon and have my hair colored again because my roots were starting to show. I hated this brown shit whenever it started to peek through the roots of my hair. I don't know why it reminded me of where I came from and who I was, but I didn't like it. I hope I can get in and out of the salon in enough time to make it to my appointment, but I knew the ins and outs of the salon. You never knew if you were going to get in and out or if you were going to have to wait around.

I dropped Tieriek at the station and continued on to the salon. I was beyond ready to have someone wash my hair. There was no feeling like the feeling when someone else washes your hair. When I walked in the salon, my stylist was already there and the shop was empty. I was grateful she hadn't booked anyone before me. I was halfway through having my locks maintained when in walked the last two people I ever wanted to see together, Nee Nee and Marshall's mother. I knew I was running the risk of running into Marshall's mother being that this was the same salon that I had first seen her in. I figured she didn't know who I was so she was no real threat, but her and Nee Nee being there together was whole different matter.

Nee Nee and I still hadn't spoken to one another since we had last seen one another at the Pavillion and we weren't on the greatest of terms. I didn't need her running her mouth right now about Marshall in front of his mother. That shit had the potential to lead my sparkly new life to an abrupt halt.

"Hey, Roxy how long are you going to be? I have another appointment I can't be late for." I whispered to Roxy who was getting ready to roll my hair up.

She popped her gum loudly. "Honey, you got at least another twenty minutes before I'm finished with your head," she said between smacking and popping her gum.

Nee Nee and Marshall's mother took a seat in the open two chairs right across from me. I swallowed hard. My eyes locked on Nee Nee and she leaned over to Marshall's mother and whispered something I couldn't hear and pointed in my direction. I knew this shit wasn't going to be good. I had to get out of there unless I wanted Nee Nee to tell Marshall's folks who I was and then they put two and two together and figured out I was the one who had had her locked up.

"Roxy, I need to use the restroom," I said nervously. I knew there was an exit out to the alley and I was going to use it. I eased out of the chair and grabbed up my purse.

"It's that time of the month," I said to Roxy. Nee Nee and Marshall's mother both had their eyes locked on me. I all but ran to the back of the salon. When I came upon the emergency exit, I snatched off the apron and threw it in the floor. I turned the knob and the alarm started to sound. As soon as I hit the alley I took off running. I looked over my shoulder and I could see Nee Nee and she was giving chase. Roxy was in the doorway screaming about me skipping out without paying her.

I was gone in the wind. I couldn't let Nee Nee catch me. Under no circumstances was I prepared to have a showdown with her. I bent the corner, digging in my purse for the keys to Tieriek's car. I was grateful for the head-start advantage I had on Nee Nee. I ran around the block to where I had parked and hopped in the car and cranked it up. I threw the car in drive and pulled off.

I had just cleared the alley I had just come from and Nee Nee appeared with a brick in her hand. She heaved the brick and it came smashing through the back window of the car. I swerved, narrowly missing another car. The driver honked his horn, clearly pissed off. I didn't give a fuck if they were mad. I was just happy I got away from Nee Nee's wrath. I threw up my middle finger at the other driver and headed in the direction of my doctor's office. Now more than ever, I needed a Vicodin. I wasn't going to let anyone ruin the night I had planned for me and Tieriek.

All News Isn't Good News

I sat in the parking lot of the physician's office trying to pull myself together. My hair was still wet
from my daring escape from the salon. I did what I
could to make myself presentable. I fussed with my hair
so I wouldn't look as crazy as I felt.

At least Roxy had colored my hair. I thought to myself.
I gave up and pulled my hair into a ponytail and exited
the car. On my way to the medical building, I got a good
look at the damage that bitch Nee Nee had done to the
car and I went from being scared to angry! I wanted to
break my foot off in her ass some kind of bad. I didn't
know how I was going to explain this shit to Tieriek. Sure,
I had some cash tucked away, but I had no intentions on
using it to get that window fixed! After all, it was his job
to take care of me. I rolled my eyes at the mess Nee Nee
had made of the car and instantly started formulating
the lie I was going to tell Tieriek.

When I got inside the doctor's office I was a few
minutes early so I flipped through some of the bridal

magazines and hoped one day real soon I would be looking through one for myself. The nurse, with her stank attitude, took her precious time with signing me in. Since she was clearly having her own issues, I sat there thirty minutes past my appointment time. When she finally called me back, I made sure I was close enough to bump into her as she held the door open. I was sick of people's shitty attitudes and I was willing to take out my frustration on anyone. This snotty bitch deserved it!

"If you don't like your job, I suggest you get another one!" I mumbled as I walked by her and into the examining room where the nurse was already waiting.

I took a seat in the chair and waited for the nurse to hand me my prescription so I could be on my way. I was already running behind, and I now had to find something to do with my hair and start dinner before picking Tieriek up. Not to mention, I had to come up with a good story to tell him about what happened to the window of the car.

"Good afternoon, Ms. Underwood. I do apologize for the wait but we were trying to obtain some information from your labs from your last visit. Dr. Crestwell will be in in a moment to talk to you about the results of some routine tests we had you take during your last visit." the nurse said. I couldn't read at what she was trying to get at. I hope she didn't have anything bad to tell me. I didn't need and couldn't handle any more surprises.

"Ma'am, I only came here to get a refill on my prescription. I normally just pick it up and go about my business. I had my other tests completed by another doctor so I know ain't nothing wrong with me," I said, growing afraid.

Had they found out I was taking the Vicodin and drinking? Did they know I sometimes took a combination of liquor, Vicodin and sleep aides to keep the nightmares away? I had all kinds of thoughts running through my mind.

"Ms. Underwood, Dr. Crestwell will be able to go over his findings in better detail," the polite woman said and there was a soft knock at the door.

"Come in," the nurse said in her cheery sing song voice. Within seconds, Dr. Crestwell entered the room.

The nurse moved over to where I was seated and took my hand. Now I was really alarmed.

"Hello, Ms. Underwood. Sorry for the long wait. Shall we get down to business?" he smiled.

I nodded my head because this whole scene was very uncomfortable. The doctor pulled out his prescription pad and I finally calmed down. Whatever they found out they could cure with medicine. So whatever was going on couldn't be that bad.

"Ms. Underwood when did you have your last menstrual cycle?"

I looked at him and tried to count back the months and I honestly couldn't remember. I couldn't even remember the last time I had even purchased a box of tampons.

I shrugged my shoulders. "I can't say I really remember," I managed to croak.

"Well, then I guess I will have to see you back here

in a couple of weeks once you have your sonogram so we can find out how far along we are." He continued to smile and wrote something on the prescription pad. He handed me two slips from the pad and stood up to leave.

I looked at the prescriptions and I didn't see anything about my Vicodin. Upon further inspection I saw the prescriptions were for a prenatal sonogram and prenatal vitamins.

"Wait. Dr. Crestwell, what are you saying?" I asked confused.

He chuckled, but I didn't see a damn thing funny. All I wanted was my Vicodin!

"Ms. Underwood, you're pregnant. How far along you are we won't know until you have the sonogram done."

He closed the door he was about to walk out of and his expression changed slightly.

"Is this pregnancy unwanted?" the doctor asked.

The nurse squeezed my hand. I wanted to snatch my hand from her and hit something. If she wasn't careful it was going to be her. There had to be a mistake. Maybe they had gotten my test results mixed up with someone else's.

"More like unexpected!" I sniffled. I didn't want to be pregnant. I wanted my medicine so I could sleep at night. I didn't come here for this.

"Well, Ms. Underwood, you have alternative options available to you. There is adoption and you do have the right to terminate the pregnancy if you wish. I would have to give you a referral if you decided to go with the latter of the two. Maybe you should go home and think on it. A good night's rest may help you make a level-headed decision. Talking to the father of the child may help you make a solid decision on your future as parents," he said warmly.

I just nodded my head. I was there, but my mind was totally gone. At the mention of getting a good night's rest I instantly started thinking about how was I going to get the Vicodin I needed now? No doctor in their right mind was going to give a pregnant woman a prescription for pain killers that strong.

"Dr. Crestwell, what about my other prescription?" I asked greedily. I was not prepared to leave his office without it. I had enough shit going on and my only solution was those pills. He had to give them to me!

"Ms. Underwood, I cannot give you anything at this time for your pain management. Until you make a decision on what you are going to do about the life you have created inside of you, I cannot give you anything more than a mild sleep sedative."

I perked up a bit and told him I wanted it. I didn't care what it was. I needed something to clear my head. He handed me a script for some over the counter shit that I am sure wasn't going to work and I left the office, more pissed off than when I had first arrived.

CHAPTER TWENTY TWO

A Baby Maybe?

I left the doctor's office and headed straight to the drug store. I filled my prenatal prescription even though I wasn't sure I was going to keep the baby. I knew Tieriek cared about me, but I didn't know how he was going to feel about bringing a baby into our relationship. It was still fresh. Even though we were playing house, I didn't know if either of us was ready for the real thing.

I managed to pull myself together enough to fix dinner and shower. By the time I had put the roast in the oven, I was worn out and ready to face the music. I didn't know how Tieriek was going to take the news about me being pregnant, but he couldn't be too upset. He was, after all, fucking me raw. So this shit was just as much his fault as it was mine for not making him use some form of protection.

The entire drive to his job was spent with me trying to concoct a lie about what happened to the back window of his car. I had gone over several different stories and I decided that I was just going to tell him I didn't see what happened. I figured the less I had to tell him the better off I would be. When I pulled up in front of the station Tieriek was already outside. He looked as good as ever in his uniform. The thoughts of making love to him entered my mind and erased the other news I had to share with him. When I got out to move to the passenger seat, I noticed Tieriek's face changed when he noticed the missing back window.

"What the hell happened to the back window?" he yelled. It caught me off guard because I had never heard Tieriek yell in the short amount of time we had been together.

I had to think of something fast because he looked like he wasn't going to move until I told him something worth him listening to.

"Baby, I don't know what happened. I went to the store to grab a few things for dinner tonight and when I came out the window was smashed in." I lied.

"Why didn't you call me and say something? Why didn't you call the police and fill out a report?" he shot back clearly pissed off about his car.

"Tieriek, I had to get to my appointment at the doctor's office that I couldn't miss. I will pay for the car to be fixed ok, just don't yell at me anymore," I said trying to conjure up some fake tears. Tieriek was all I had in this world and I didn't want him angry with me.

"Wait, what did you go to the doctor for, is everything alright?"

I batted my blue eyes at him and let the fake tears fall hoping to gain some sympathy from him. "Tieriek, that

POWDER

is what I wanted to talk to you about. Can we go home first? I don't want to have this conversation out here in front of your job."

He didn't utter another word. He got in the driver's seat and slammed the door so hard the jagged pieces of glass that was hanging from the back window fell loose from the frame and caused him to tense up.

I slid into the passenger seat and stared straight ahead, too afraid to say anything else. When we got home, I rushed around and set the table for dinner. Tieriek still hadn't said anything to me. Instead, he headed straight up the stairs and I heard the shower come alive.

I sat down at the kitchen table and tried to figure out how I was going to drop this major bombshell on him. If Tieriek was this angry about a car, there was no telling what he would do about me being pregnant.

He finally joined me at the table and sat down. "Now, what did you go to the doctor for? Are you ok?" Tieriek asked, digging into his pork roast, mashed potatoes, cornbread, and collard greens. He stuffed a forkful of food in his mouth and stared at me intently.

"Well, I went in to have a follow-up appointment about my injuries and I found out that I am pregnant," I blurted out.

There was no beating around the bush about the issue I decided this was something I hadn't done to myself and I wasn't going to take responsibility for our actions by myself either.

Tieriek dropped the fork in his plate and stared at me.

"Are you serious? I mean we're going to be parents?" he smiled widely.

He pushed his chair away from the table and kneeled down where I was seated. "Samantha, you have made me the happiest man in the world. I know I lost my temper earlier, but that shit doesn't mean anything. The car can be fixed. Don't worry about it. I will take care of it in the morning," Tieriek said with so much sincerity my heart fluttered.

"So, you want this baby? I mean this is ok with you?" I sniffled through watery eyes.

"Ok? This is better than ok! This is the best thing that has ever happened to me. I told you before that all I wanted was you. Now I have another reason to love you," Tieriek said.

"Now, all we have to do to make this official is for us to start planning our wedding!"

"What? You want to marry me? You don't have to marry me just because I'm pregnant; you know."

"Samantha, I'm not marrying you just because you're having my baby. I'm marrying you because I knew from the first day I met you, that you were the one. I don't want to be without you and I definitely don't want just a baby momma'. I want the whole thing! The family, the kids... everything as long as I have you!"

I was speechless. The whole time I thought he was going to hate me as much as I hated myself for getting pregnant. That wasn't the case. He was really excited about the whole thing. I'm not so sure how I felt about it yet, but somewhere in the back of my mind my greed took over. I needed someone to take care of me and if I had to have this baby to ensure that would happen, then I would do so. I loved Tieriek, but I wasn't sure it was for the right reasons. I think it was for the security and stability. I felt like he could protect me. That alone made the words fall from my lips.

"Yes! I will marry you Tieriek!" I gushed.

He stood up and pulled me to my feet. We kissed long and deep. I could feel his nature rising and thumping my thigh. Tieriek's hand moved down between my creamy thighs. I knew what he wanted and I was going to give it to him.

Despite all of the shit that happened earlier today, I guess my day wasn't as bad as I thought after all.

WWW.GSTREETCHRONICLES.COM

CHAPTER TWENTY-THREE

New Beginnings

Tieriek and I were on our way to my first sonogram appointment. He was so geeked up about the baby. That's all he seemed to want to talk about. Everything was *his son* this and *his son* that.

I was just getting used to the idea of having a baby and he had already picked out names for the kid and we still didn't know how far along I was, let alone the sex of the baby. Tieriek was so sure it was a boy. I, on the other hand, didn't care if it was a boy or a girl as long as it was healthy. Maybe it wasn't such a bad idea having this baby because I hadn't had one nightmare since I found out I was pregnant and Tieriek said I was glowing. I was barely showing, but I could tell already that this was going to be a big baby. I already started sporting a small baby bump, but you couldn't really tell.

I was excited and nervous about being a parent. I didn't want to be the kind of parent my parents were, so I decided I wouldn't take anything stronger than a Tylenol. I can't lie and say I didn't miss the soothing effects of my beloved Vicodin, but if it could hurt the baby and possibly fuck up my future with Tieriek then I wasn't going to take any chances.

We drove along, chatting about the wedding we were planning. We didn't want to have anything too big because it would just be some of Tieriek's family and friends. The truth was I didn't have anyone to invite. I wasn't going to invite my parents because I didn't want them embarrassing me and they would most likely be somewhere too high to give a damn about me, a wedding, or a baby.

Tieriek asked me about them while we were thinking of who we should inform about our union and the pregnancy. I made up some shit about them being killed in a car accident. I didn't want him to know they were junkies that were probably too doped up to comprehend what was taking place in my new life. I had all but forgotten about them. I would rather leave their sorry asses in the past, so telling Tieriek they were dead was for the best. My parents had no place in my life anyway.

We were waiting to have the sonogram done when my cell phone started ringing. It caught me off guard because no one had the number since I changed it. No one called me but Tieriek and since we were together I was sure the caller had the wrong number.

"Hello."

No one said anything, so I assumed the caller had the wrong number as I expected. Just as I was putting the phone away in my bag, it rang again. The number was blocked as before. I figured just like before it was the same party calling back.

"Hello?" I said into this phone.

This time I could hear someone on the other end breathing. I went to swipe the end but on the screen and someone finally spoke.

"I told you not to play with me bitch! I am going to kill off everyone you love...one by one!"

Then the line went dead. All of the color drained from my face. My usual rosy glow was nonexistent. Tieriek noticed the change in my demeanor.

"Baby, is everything ok? You look like you saw a ghost."

"I'm fine. I just feel queasy all of a sudden. I guess it's a pregnancy thing or something," I tried to reason.

He squeezed my hand and offered to get my some water. I needed a minute to think so I told him that would probably help. He went down to the gift shop while I sat there trying to understand how Adekite had gotten my new number. I shuddered at the thought of him finding me. I had to straighten up before Tieriek returned. I couldn't let him know anything about Adekite or Katavious. That was on a *need-to-know* basis and Tieriek definitely didn't need to know about them!

As soon as I knew Tieriek was out of sight, I rushed to the bathroom and threw up. I didn't think it was the morning sickness causing my stomach to ball up in knots. It was the phone call that had me nervous and just about ready to jump out of my skin. I knew that voice anywhere. There was no mistaking that it was Adekite. I flushed cool water on my face and tried to control my rattled nerves. Once we got out of here I was going to change the number again. I was baffled about how Adekite was able to get it, but I reasoned that maybe my number was listed as public. I was going to make sure this time I had it changed and no one had access to it. I was going to have it marked as private. I would have gotten rid of the damn thing if it weren't for Tieriek insisting that I kept it on at all times. He said it was so if I ever had an emergency he would only be a phone call away. Now I was starting to think that wasn't such a good idea. I knew me getting rid of the phone altogether wasn't going to happen, so I would have to think of a lie to tell him about why I changed the number.

Once I had shaken off some of the bad vibes from the phone call, I returned to my seat in the waiting room. When Tieriek returned, he was carrying a bag full of peppermint and a bottle of Avian and he was wearing a strange look on his face. He handed the bag of mints and the water to me and I smiled weakly.

"What's up with the mints?" I asked him. I hated peppermint. They reminded me of my childhood. I used to steal them from the corner store. They were the only things I had enough balls to take when I was younger and I only took them because I didn't have a choice. My parents didn't put food in the house, so on many nights I sucked on the stolen candies to quiet my hunger.

"Oh, the lady in the gift shop said they would help with the morning sickness. Samantha, who called your phone before I left?"

I could see his whole demeanor had changed and he

POWDER

looked uncomfortable.

"It was a wrong number. Why?" I said twisting the cap off of the water and avoiding his inquiring stare.

"I was asking because I just got a weird phone call."

I almost choked on the water I was now sipping.

"You got a weird phone call? What did he say?" I asked nervously looking around.

"The caller said that I had better watch my ass and that bitch, Powder, was as good as dead," he said staring at me.

I dropped the entire bottle of water on the floor with the mention of my alias, Powder. Tieriek knew nothing about my nickname. The only people who knew about my street name were people from my past and they should not be contacting me, let alone contacting Tieriek. I played it off as best as I could. "I wonder who that could be. Sure glad that I ain't her." I laughed.

"How did you know the caller was a he? I never said anything about who had called me, I just repeated what they said." Tieriek looked at me curiously.

I shifted around uncomfortably. "I guess I assumed it was a he. I don't know what's going on, I'm just as confused by your phone call as you are."

"Mr. and Mrs. Kern, the doctor is ready for the two for you now." The receptionist interrupted our uncomfortable conversation and I was glad for the distraction. I also loved the way the receptionist addressed me as Mrs. Kern. I was a step closer to leaving my dirty little past in the past.

We headed into the back and I got undressed. The

technician put a huge glob of the cold jelly on my belly and moved the wand over my stomach. He had turned the screen so that Tieriek and I could see what our creation inside my womb was doing, and I was shocked when I saw two little shadows the size of golf balls moving around inside.

"Well, mom and dad, it looks like you have two bundles of joy in there instead of just one. Mrs. Kern you are having twins. From the looks of it, you are about three months out. We will get you scheduled for another sonogram in two months to check their progress and we should be able to tell the sex of the babies at that time too, and nail down a better due date. Being that you have twins there is a high possibility that you won't make it all the way through your pregnancy without early labor. You shouldn't worry about that because almost every pregnant woman with twins goes into early labor. I'm sure your OB/GYN will give you more information."

Tieriek was focused on the screen and I could see the excitement written all over his face. I, on the other hand, was in shock. There wasn't just one life I was going to be responsible for, but two. I guess that explains why I was starting to pick up so much weight so fast.

The technician left the room and Tieriek kissed my forehead. "Baby, everything about you is so amazing! You never cease to amaze me, Samantha. We're having twins! Can you believe it?"

I stared at the pictures that the technician gave us. I was going to be a mother of two little people and I was going to marry an incredible man. Maybe God did forgive me for all of the horrible things I had done in my recent past. He was giving me another chance to make up for all the wrong I had done.

My Daughter's Hand In Marriage

The months zoomed by and the doctor put me on bed rest around my sixth month of pregnancy. The strain of carrying the babies was wearing me out. With each passing day, I grew more and more excited about their arrival. We found out about a month ago that Tieriek was getting his boy and we were also having a little girl too. I was ecstatic. Tieriek was beyond elated and was anxiously awaiting their arrival. He spent all of his free time catering to my needs and being the great man that he had already proven himself to be.

Since I had been put on bed rest Tieriek and I decided that we were going to hold off until they were born before we had the wedding. I was in no condition to say, "I Do" although I was more than ready to do so. Instead, I spent my final days of pregnancy preparing for my baby shower. Tieriek had invited all of his co-workers from the force, including his partner Officer Shiloh. I still didn't like her and I know the feeling was mutual. I think her real problem was that she was jealous that

I had snagged Tieriek, and I know she was only hostile about it because I was white and he didn't want her! I could tell she had issues with me since the day I had met her. I could also tell that she had more than just casual feelings for Tieriek. I didn't care how she felt about him as long as she didn't overstep her boundaries.

* * * * *

The day of the shower I was beyond excited to see what everyone had gotten the babies. Tieriek took the liberty of decorating the entire house and everything was beautiful. I swear I am the luckiest woman in the world.

Tieriek had run out to pick up the last minute things for the shower when the doorbell rang. I wobbled down the stairs to answer it. I figured it was one of the guests who had arrived early for the shower. I opened the door and was greeted by a DHL driver carrying a gift wrapped box. The box was addressed to Mrs. Kern and I was eager to see what was inside. I signed off on the delivery and inspected the card. The card didn't say who the gift was from.

The card read:

A little preview of what's to come! Sorry I could not be at your shower, but I will be seeing you soon.

I took the box to the backyard where the gift table was set up. We had picked a beautiful day to have the shower. It was early Fall, so the temperature was perfect for such a perfect occasion. I went about making sure everything was in order before the guests really arrived.

I didn't want anything to be out of place. I showered and dressed in a soft yellow Hailey maternity dress, and took my phone downstairs just in enough time to catch Tieriek walking in the door with Officer Shiloh following closely behind him. When she saw me, she didn't acknowledge me. She headed straight to the backyard and didn't bother to speak to me at all. If I wasn't pregnant I would have smacked her disrespectful ass. I didn't know what her issue was with me, but she had better get over it because I wasn't going anywhere and as long as she was Tieriek's partner, she was going to have to deal with me to a certain extent.

I grabbed Tieriek by his arm and pulled him to the side.

"Look, baby, today is supposed to be about you, me and the babies. I don't know what your partner has against me, but I will not tolerate her behavior. So either you better check that hoe or I will!" I said with my hands planted firmly on my hips.

Tieriek chuckled at my statement, but I didn't see a damn thing funny. "You ain't checking nobody Sam, so save all the drama. We have a baby shower to attend so whatever beef you and my partner have with one another needs to be put on the back burner. I want this day to be unforgettable for us. I want you to relax and enjoy yourself," he said, cupping my chin in his hands and giving me a peck on my lips.

Our kiss was interrupted by the sound of the doorbell. "You ready?" he asked me.

I nodded my head and headed for the backyard to

take my seat in the chair that was decorated in pink balloons and streamers. I had to admit the shower was beautiful. The food was delicious and the cake was to die for. Our guests played the traditional baby shower games and enjoyed themselves. When it was time to open the gifts, Tieriek and I opened hundreds of boxes with two of everything. Everything we received in blue we would receive an identical item in pink.

When we got to the last box, which was the one that was delivered, I handed it to Tieriek for him to open. I figured he might as well because it had to come from one of his friends or co-workers who couldn't attend the shower. Tieriek opened the card and shrugged his broad shoulders and pulled the bow from the top of the box and tossed it to the side. He carefully unwrapped the box and found there was another card inside. Tieriek opened the card and read it aloud for all of his guests to hear.

"Officer Kern, maybe you should ask her father for her hand in marriage," he said smiling. He shrugged again and dug through the box and pulled out what looked like a hand that had been chopped off at the wrist.

"What kind of sick shit is this? Who the fuck brought this gift here? Who sent this shit?" He yelled at his guests that were all in awe of the horror unfolding in front of them.

I knew who sent that box and I knew just whose hand that was that Tieriek had dropped on the lawn. I understood what the card meant and I knew what it all meant for me. Adekite had found me. But what was even more astonishing was the fact that he had found my parents. I knew that cryptic message about asking my father's hand in marriage was sick and sadistic.

That is when I felt it. My stomach contracted and I heaved up everything I ate during the party. There was confusion all around me. Tieriek's co-workers were doing what their police officer instincts told them to do. They were scrambling around and no one seemed to notice that I was in extreme pain until I dropped on my knees and cradled my stomach that was being rocked with tremors. Tieriek noticed I was on the ground and tried to help me up. I couldn't move. That's when I felt the hot liquid stream down my legs and I screamed out from the pain.

"Oh, my God, someone call an ambulance. I think Samantha is going into labor!"

I was hyperventilating and rolling around in pain. After what seemed like an eternity, the ambulance arrived and transported me to the hospital where they admitted me. The doctors were all running around prepping me for an emergency delivery. Tieriek held my hand and stroked my hair.

"Baby, it's going to be ok. I'm right here."

I nodded my head. That was all I could do because another contraction rocked my abdomen violently. Once the contraction subsided, I was able to speak through the tears that were spilling from my lids.

"Oh, God, Tieriek, are the babies going to be alright? Are they going to make it? I don't know what I will do if something happens to them. I'm sorry, baby. I'm so sorry! I didn't mean for any of this to happen." I cried. I sucked in as much air as I could as another contraction shook me to my core.

"Samantha, don't be crazy. None of this is your fault. There was no way you could have known what was in that box. I swear to God, I will hunt down the person responsible for this. I will make whatever mutha' fucka' did this pay!" He whispered to me before the nurses whisked him away to get scrubbed and changed for the delivery.

Exactly one hour later, Marcella Kern and Tieriek Kern Jr. were born. Marcella weighed three pounds and four ounces and Tieriek weighed in at four pounds even. From what the nurses said, they were both fighters. They had to be put on respirators because their lungs weren't fully developed, but the doctors were confident in their chance of making it. I was still concerned because they were both so little...I could hold them in my hand. That is, if they had allowed me to hold them. Once I was strong enough to be wheeled to the NICU, I had to wonder if my children were going to make it and I couldn't even hold them. Although the doctors said what happened was a combination of shock and Toxemia that triggered my labor, I knew better than that. They were fighting for their lives and it was all my fault.

Tieriek never left my side, just like he promised, but I had no words for him or anyone else. I refused to speak to anyone and the doctors said I was suffering from a combination of Post Traumatic Syndrome and Shock. That wasn't it at all! My guilt was eating me alive. I had done some horrible shit in my short life, but nothing could compare to this. My greed almost killed my babies.

Tieriek stayed in touch with his job to see if anyone had any leads on what happened. I knew he had a million and one questions for me, but he could save that shit because I didn't have anything to say. Tieriek said that we were definitely moving because if whomever sent that box knew where we lived, they could easily come back and do something far worse. I didn't see how anything could be worse than receiving a hand in a box on the day of your baby shower.

I guess what was so fucked up about it was that I couldn't tell Tieriek whose hand I believed it was. I didn't know how to tell him that the cryptic riddle about *asking her father for her hand in marriage* was for me. Adekite had done something horrible to my father and possibly my mother. I can't say I was saddened about what he may have done to them, but my heart was breaking for what he had almost done to my children. They weren't out of the woods yet, so their wellbeing was all I could think about.

Tieriek had excused himself to take a phone call. It had something to do with his realtor and property that we could move into right away. Tieriek had cashed in his 401k and his pension to make the move happen at the speed he was doing it. I overheard him saying that he would get his money back once the old house sold and he would put the money back. I couldn't help but think that I was a lucky woman.

I was happy that Tieriek had stepped out. I felt

somewhat smothered with him being right there in the room with me. I pushed the call button and the nurse entered. I asked her for something for pain. When she returned she had a little plastic medicine cup, and a Styrofoam cup with water. The sight of the pills made my mouth water. I needed some rest because this whole ordeal was crazy and I knew it was far from over.

By the time Tieriek had re-entered the room I was drifting into a drug-induced haze and loving it. I heard him say something to the nurse about leaving and returning. The way the pain medicine had me feeling, I didn't care about anything he was talking about.

The next thing I knew I was pulled into a thousand dreams.

A Taste of War

I went home two weeks after the babies were born.
I can't say I was happy about returning to the real
world. The real world didn't have a call button where
a nurse would come running to bring me medicine.
Tieriek did everything in his power to make going home
without the babies easy for me. I hated to leave them in
the hospital, but they were still in no shape to leave when
I was released. The doctors said they would probably
be in the NICU until they were able to breathe on their
own, which would be about another two months.

I guess it was best that they were safe in the hospital
and Adekite couldn't touch them. Tieriek had taken the
liberty of moving us into a three-bedroom, three-bath
townhome in the suburbs of Maryland. The further I
was from DC the better off I figured we would be, but
I still worried about Adekite finding us. Maryland was
nothing but a hop, skip and a jump from DC.

I still didn't have much to say about anything and
Tieriek didn't seem like he was going to force me to

talk about the incident. Once I was released from the hospital and was brought to our new home, Tieriek let me know he had missed enough time from work and that he would be heading in to his job. He asked me over and over again was I alright with being alone. I answered him with my usual nods. I still didn't have anything to say to him. My guilt was eating me alive.

Once he left for the day, I turned on the television and the first thing that caught my attention was the news. The reporter was updating the public on Breaking News live out of S.E. Washington DC. I turned the television up and paid close attention.

This just in. The bodies of two, unidentified, middle-aged people were found in this local neighborhood after neighbors complained about a very foul odor coming from the residence behind me.

The camera panned out to the house and I froze in horror when I saw the familiar rundown house.

Police were called to the scene, which is now being ruled a double homicide. The badly decomposing bodies of what appeared to be one white male and one white female were found inside the home. The police described the scene as sickening and shockingly disturbing. The male victim appeared to have had his hand chopped off at the wrist and the police are combing the area to see if they are able to find any more clues as to what occurred here.

I cut the television off and cried. I didn't cry because my parents were dead. I cried because I knew Adekite was going to come for me, and I was afraid. I didn't care if I had a police officer for a fiancé. Adekite had already proved that he was going to find me, and when he did, it was going to be lights out. I don't think I could put enough miles between us to feel safe. I wanted to get my stuff and get the hell out of the DMV, but I didn't want to leave my babies behind. Although I loved Tieriek, I kept telling myself I could walk away from him if I needed to, but my children...I couldn't leave behind. They were the only reason I hadn't packed my shit the moment Tieriek walked out the door to head to work and never looked back. I couldn't abandon them, they needed me and I felt like I needed them to keep me from falling apart.

My cell phone rang and I scooped it up and saw it was a blocked call. Seeing that the caller didn't want me to know their number made the hair on the back of my neck stand up. Tieriek had not only given me a new phone and number, but he had also changed the cell phone carrier. He did that after he had received the call in the doctor's office a few months back. There was no way anyone had this new number. Hell, I could barely remember it.

"Hello," I answered nervously into the phone.

"I hope you enjoyed your gift. Believe me, Samantha, the fun ain't over yet." There was laughter and the line went dead. I felt lightheaded. I heaved up my breakfast and cried. For the first time I realized how fucked up my situation really was. There was no out running Adekite. He wasn't ever going to let me live peacefully. I had stolen from him and that was all he cared about. He was hell bent on revenge.

After crying for half of the morning, I called Tieriek and told him that I didn't feel safe in this new house by myself. He assured me that everything was going to be fine and that he would send over one of his fellow boys in blue to keep a watch on me and the house. There was no way for Tieriek to understand my fear. He didn't know what I had subjected our family to. He didn't know anything about my checkered past. Even if I started trying to explain today, he would either not understand why I had done so many things to so many people and would leave me; or he would swear he could fix everything and get his head blown off trying to defend us.

"Karma is a bitch!" I mumbled to myself. I gathered my thoughts and decided that I wanted to go back to the hospital and see my babies. They kept me focused. They were the only cure for my depression. Just being around Marcella and Tieriek Jr. soothed me.

I spent the entire day at the hospital with the babies. I didn't want to miss one minute of being in their lives. The babies had to stay in the hospital for another month and a half before they were evaluated and hopefully they would be released. The doctors said they would only come home once they were able to breathe on their own and gained a few more pounds. I was hopeful that my children were going to make it through this ordeal. They were my children, so I knew they were nothing but survivors. Just like me. No matter how much they resembled their dad, they were my little soldiers; and they had no idea that I had introduced them to their first taste of war the moment they were born.

CHAPTER
TWENTY SIX

Karma is a Bitch and Payback is a Motherfucka'

After moving to the new house I never felt safe there and it caused plenty of arguments between me and Tieriek. Where we had never had a disagreement before, we were now constantly at each other's throats. I was still being cold and callous towards him, and the only people I showed any affection towards were the twins. I guess my behavior was starting to wear thin and Tieriek and I barely said more than three words per day to one another; which was fine by me. I didn't have shit to say to him if it didn't involve the children. I was starting to think being with him was a mistake.

Today was just like any other day since the kids had been born. I was preparing to go to the hospital and sit with the babies, they were going to be released today and I didn't want to miss out on another second of their little lives. It pained me each time I had to leave the hospital and I couldn't take my children with me. No mother should ever have to endure that kind of pain.

Tieriek and I had fussed about why I had to be at the

hospital before the kids were discharged. I called him an insensitive bastard and told him he had better take me to my children unless he wanted to feel my wrath. To avoid further argument, he decided not to protest and do as I had wished. He dropped me at the hospital and he went about his business. He had dropped me, the matching car seats, and baby bags at the entrance and peeled off. I threw up my middle finger at him as he turned the corner. He was really working my nerves. He didn't even bother to help me carry the babies' belongings inside the hospital before he sped off to do whatever it was that he did when he wasn't with me.

I was starting to suspect that he and that bitch, Officer Shiloh, were more than partners; but whenever I would bring it up, he would brush it off and act as though I were making shit up to get under his skin. It wasn't uncommon for me to come home from visiting the twins and Officer Shiloh and Tieriek would be posted up in the house like they didn't have a care in the world.

I decided that I wasn't going to waste my time on worrying about what Tieriek and that *she devil* were up to. I wasn't going to let anything get in the way of this joyous occasion. My babies were coming home with me today, and if nothing else, I was happy about that. God had not only spared their lives despite all of the despicable shit I had done, but He was going to allow me to watch my children grow up.

The nurses gave the children their baths and I assisted them with the feedings as I had done on my many visits. I packed up all of their things in their respective bags and waited. Once the doctor gave my children the *all clear* I felt like the happiest woman in the world. I hadn't felt this way since before they were born. Not since Tieriek asked me to marry him.

I waited on Tieriek for over an hour. Then I began calling him and his phone was going straight to voicemail. I started thinking wild shit. I knew he was probably somewhere laid up with that bitch, Shiloh, and that normally would have sent me into a blind rage, but not today. I was too amped up about my babies coming home with me.

I had finally made a realization that no matter what... my children would love me. I vowed to never be the type of parent my parents were to me, and that my children were going to be the center of my universe no matter what their father was up to. I assisted the nurses with dressing the children and I decided to try calling Tieriek one more time. I was sent straight to the voicemail... again. This time I sounded off on his voicemail and gave him a piece of my mind. I called a cab and proceeded to take the children home on my own.

By the time the children and I pulled up in front of the house I was furious. Tieriek's car was out front, but so was Shiloh's. I paid the cabbie and put the baby bags over my shoulders, crisscross style, and headed up the steps. I sniffed the air and smelled the faint smell of barbecue, which was odd because it was the middle of November and damn near thirty degrees outside. Unless someone was tailgating, no one should have been crazy enough to be outside in this kind of weather.

The night before there was snow in the forecast and to my knowledge there was no football on Thursdays.

I managed to unlock the front door and get the children in out of the cold. Marcella was fast asleep and Tieriek was in his seat fussing like there was no tomorrow. Once we were inside, I called Tieriek's name and there was no answer. I noticed the house was very dark for it to be the middle of the day. Something seemed out of place, but I couldn't put my finger on it.

I placed the car seat with Marcella on the couch and removed Tieriek Jr. from his seat since he didn't seem to let up with his fussing. I cradled him in my arms to quiet him. I roamed through the rest of the house looking for Tieriek. I checked everywhere and he, nor that bitch, Officer Shiloh, were anywhere to be found. My anger with Tieriek quickly dissolved and turned to fear as I searched from room to room looking for him. My search led me back to the living room where I had left Marcella sleeping in her car seat. Tieriek Jr. had fallen asleep in my arms and I placed him back in his seat next to his sister; who was sleeping peacefully.

I stood in the dark living room trying to figure out where Tieriek was. It didn't make sense that his car was parked out front and Shiloh's cruiser was parked at the curb. I went over to the sliding glass window that lead to the patio and opened the curtains to let the sunlight in. That is when I noticed two things that were out of place. There was a huge pool of blood and shreds of clothing that were thrown about the backyard and patio. My eyes travelled from the pool of blood and clothing to the grill that was smoking something fierce. The lit grill explained why I had smelled barbecue when the cabbie had dropped me and the babies off. I looked over my shoulder at the kids who were both asleep.

I cautiously slid the glass door open and upon further inspection, I noticed the shredded clothes were the shirt that Tieriek had on when he dropped me off at the hospital. The other ripped clothing looked like a blue police officers uniform. My heart thundered in my chest as I stepped onto the patio, careful to avoid the pools of blood that were staining the cold concrete.

"Tieriek! This shit isn't funny! Will you please answer me!" I yelled. I could hear something sizzling and popping on the grill. I inched closer to the over-sized grill and took a deep breath before lifting the heavy top. As I opened the grill, black smoke poured out. Once the cool Fall breeze swept the plumes of smoke away and I was able to see just what was cooking on the grill, a scream so deafening escaped my lips.

I was face to face with my fiancé' and his partner's charred remains. They had both been cut up and put on the grill. I screamed for what felt like an eternity. I screamed until I was hoarse and I couldn't scream anymore. The pain I felt for my fiancé was immeasurable. I turned to run back into the house and slammed the patio door behind me once inside. I closed my eyes and cried. I knew karma had caught up to me and was making me pay big time for everything I had done in my past.

I heard movement and my eyes flew open to see my

nightmares coming to life. That is when I saw her. Nee Nee was standing in my living room with my newborn son in her arms and she was brandishing a knife in her free hand.

"Well, hello Powder. You look surprised to see me," she chuckled.

"Nee Nee, what are you doing here? Give me my baby!" I demanded between sobs.

Her smile widened and my stomach turned. I knew she was the one responsible for Tieriek and Shiloh cooking to a crisp on the grill.

"Oh, so you give a fuck about someone other than yourself now; huh? Funny, you didn't seem to care when you were killing Marshall. You didn't give a fuck when you had his mother locked up on some bogus shit that you knew she ain't have shit to do with. Tell me something, Powder, why should I give a fuck about you or this bastard baby?" she said holding the knife to Tieriek Jr.'s neck.

I was glued to one spot. I was trying to figure out how I was going to get out of this. I was desperate to get my son from this mad woman. I looked over at the car seat where I had left Marcella and noticed she wasn't where I left her.

"Nee Nee, where is my daughter? Please, don't hurt my babies." I begged. "Look, I'm sorry for everything. I know sorry doesn't fix it, but hurting my children won't fix it either. Where is my daughter? Why are you doing this to me? My family didn't do anything to deserve this, Nee Nee." I cried.

I heard Marcella's muffled cries and I knew Nee Nee wasn't in my home alone. I looked up to see Adekite walk calmly into the room with a smile plastered across his face. My blood ran cold and I turned into a blubbering mess when I saw him. He was joined by his brothers Katavious and Ohruh, followed by Rasaun who was holding Marcella's body in his arms. I knew they were not going to let me walk out of there and the only thing I could do was beg for the lives of my children. I decided to try to plead to the only one of the deadly group who may have had some compassion for me and everything that was happening, Ohruh.

"Ohruh, please don't let them hurt my children. They didn't do anything to deserve any of this. Please!" I begged over and over. Ohruh couldn't look at me, so I knew if I could talk some sense into him I may have had a fighting chance. Ohruh lowered his eyes to the floor and shook his head.

"Sorry, Powder. I told you not to fuck with my brother. I told you he wasn't to be fucked with and you didn't listen," Ohruh said. I could see the sorrow in his eyes and I knew my pleas were falling on deaf ears. There was no talking any of them down.

"Bitch, no one wants to hear your sob stories! You killed my best friend! You gave him a hot dose to get rid of him and we're supposed to feel sorry for you! You ain't shit, but the child of junkies. You ain't never have shit until Marshall saved your trashy white ass and you repaid him by killing him!" Rasaun spat.

"Rasaun, that's not what happened! Adekite made

BlaQue

me do it. Did he tell you he was the one who gave me the hot dose? I bet he didn't tell you that; did he?" I screamed.

"Enough of this shit! Do it and get this shit over with!" Adekite ordered.

I knew Adekite wanted to have me silenced before I could tell Rasaun and Nee Nee what had really gone down with Marshall. He was using them to do his dirty work. That was so typical of Adekite. He would give orders, but was never the one to pull the trigger... so to speak. He did it with Marshall and now he was manipulating Nee Nee and Rasaun to do the same thing.

"With pleasure!" Nee Nee smiled. She took the knife and slid it deep across my sleeping son's neck and dropped him to the floor like he was a piece of trash. He didn't even have a chance to cry out. I broke down after seeing my son laying there with his head partially detached from his body. I dropped to my knees and sobbed for my son who never had a fighting chance against this band of hellions who were hell bent on revenge. I took my gaze away from the heap on the floor that was my son and started to beg for Marcella's life. Adekite acted like he didn't hear me. He just smiled and nodded in Rasaun's direction.

Rasaun snapped Marcella's neck and tossed her to the floor next to Tieriek Jr. There was no reason to live anymore. I had done so much dirt that it had all caught up to me. I wasn't going to walk away from this mess I created.

Really why would they let me walk away? They had

taken the lives of four innocent people. Two of which were officers of the law. I knew they were not going to be gracious enough to let me live. What they didn't know is that by letting me live would have been punishment enough. I would have to live with the fact that I had caused my entire family to be slain. I would rather they killed me. If I couldn't have my children and Tieriek there was no reason to live this life.

These thugs had stolen the only man who had loved me and murdered my children in cold blood in front of me. I didn't have anything else left.

Adekite stepped closer to me and turned to his partners in crime and ordered for them to get out. When his posse had left my house, Adekite pulled a gun from his waistband with a silencer attached and aimed it at my chest. I guess I had misjudged him. I knew he was ruthless, but before I had seen him pull out the gun I thought he never got his hands dirty with shit like this. I thought he was only good for giving orders. I guess I was wrong.

My heart was broken in a million pieces looking at my children lying dead on the floor in front of me. I wanted nothing more than to join them so I could tell them that I was sorry for the pain I had caused them in the little bit of time they were on this earth. I wanted to tell them how much I loved them. I closed my eyes and prayed to God for His forgiveness because I knew this was it. If I begged God for forgiveness maybe He would grant me a chance to see Tieriek and my children in heaven.

"Oh, by the way you shady bitch, this whole thing

would have been much worse if I hadn't gotten my money back. I would have killed your sorry ass long ago if customs wouldn't have found the luggage with my brother's travel documents that you had stolen inside and returned my money to me!

I thought I told you before that I was the king of this jungle and there isn't enough room for me and you here!" Adekite smiled and pulled the trigger.

My body hit the floor. I just wanted the burning sensation in my chest to cease. My body was growing cold and I wanted nothing more than to just die so I could be with the only people I had ever given a damn about; my children and Tieriek.

From my position on the floor, and barely conscious, I saw Adekite walk out. He stopped right before he got to the front door and started having a conversation with someone. I could only tell the voice belonged to a woman.

"She's all yours. I left her alive, I think." I heard Adekite joke and then I saw his feet cross the threshold to exit through the front door. I wanted to scream out, I wanted someone to make the intense pain in my chest stop, but I was afraid to raise my head. The footfalls of who I assumed was the woman that Adekite had been speaking with stopped right in front of where I was bleeding to death in my living room floor.

"Look at me bitch!" the woman's voice demanded.

I was paralyzed with fear and I was in no shape to move. Had I moved, I knew the pain of the bullet that was bouncing around somewhere in my chest would move and cause more pain.

"Oh, so you don't want to look at me when I am speaking; huh? I told my son to leave you trashy bitches alone. I don't know where he got you from, but little lady, you caused a whole lot of trouble, but it ends here and it ends today!" the woman laughed.

I struggled to turn my head towards the familiar voice and when I was able to get it into a position where I could see who was really calling the shots I could have died from disbelief.

It was Marshall's mother. She was dressed to the nines and she was glaring down at me with a revolver in her hand.

"You piece of white trash, I should have killed you when you had me locked up. I told Adekite to let me kill you, but you know how he is. He wants to control everything. Ole' selfish bastard. That's why I am gonna murder his ass right after I finish with you. I told my son not to fuck with you gutter bitches, but he never listened to anything I said. Had he listened to his dear old mother he would be alive right now. He just had to fuck with you; didn't he? I told him be wise about the company he keeps and look where that got him. It led him to an early grave. Had he listened to me when I tried to help him and get him into a rehab, he would be alive. But noooooo...he just had to have his token white bitch and now he is gonna have your sorry ass alongside him in hell!"

Marshall's mother stooped down careful not to get her gleaming white, floor-length coat dirty with the blood that was leaking from my chest. She pushed the barrel of the gun in my face and pulled the trigger.

The last thing I remembered before I drifted into the realm of the dead was thinking that karma was a bitch, and payback was a motherfucka', and neither of them discriminated because of the color of your skin.

BLAQUE

The Authoress BlaQue, nicknamed the BlaQue Angel because of the twisted and dark stories she weaves, was born and raised in the Washington, D.C. area where she currently resides with her son.

BlaQue began writing after reading several Donald Goines books and decided she would love to pen stories in the same gritty, fast-paced manner. After writing her first novel Dirty DNA and allowing several of her peers to read and critique her work, she decided to submit it to G Street Chronicles where she joined the ranks of some of the heaviest hitting authors in Urban Literature.

We'd like to thank you for supporting G Street Chronicles and invite you to join our social networks.
Please be sure to post a review when you're finished reading.

Like us on Facebook
G Street Chronicles
G Street Chronicles CEO Exclusive Readers Group

Follow us on Twitter
@GStreetChronicl

Follow us on Instagram
gstreetchronicles

Email us and we'll add you to our mailing list
fans@gstreetchronicles.com

George Sherman Hudson, CEO
Shawna A., COO